Adrenaline

A Novella

By

Kya Aliana

For Jennifer

Happy Reading

—Kya Aliana

This book is dedicated to my Grandad – thank you for all the amazing memories you've given me. You've taught me so much and have always been there for me to talk to you about anything. Your undying support has helped me accomplish what before I could only dream of. Thank you for everything. I love you.
Happy Birthday!

This is a work of fiction. Any similarities between characters and actual people are purely coincidental. All places, characters, events, and actions in this novella are figments of the author's wild and rampant imagination.

Cover art photo by: rc

Cover art design by: Kya Aliana

Cover art modeling by: Lexi Cranor

Interior text design by: Kya Aliana

10 9 8 7 6 5 4 3 2 1

First Edition

First Printing: March 2013

No proof copies of this novella were made.

ISBN: 978-1482782356

PRINTED IN THE UNITED STATES OF AMERICA

Chapter One
Adrenaline

"What the fuck was that?" he asks, breaking our kiss.

"I told you I don't like it when you cuss," I say, sitting up and looking around the night. I hear it too. I hear it scurry over to my side. I look at Bentley, but he doesn't see me. His head is turned the other way. Even without looking at his face, I know his eyes are frantically searching for something... anything that seems out of the ordinary. I know he's scared. He doesn't handle fear as well as I do. I suppose that I handle it better because I read more horror than he does. But then again, it makes me awful jumpy sometimes when I really do get freaked out. The full moon lights the graveyard enough to make out the far and few between tombstones. It's a fresh graveyard, which gives it a more and less eerie feeling at the same time.

"It was probably just a squirrel, love," I say, pressing my chest up against his back and wrapping my arms around his neck. He looks back at me and kisses my cheek.

"Are you sure there's nothing out there?" he asks, running his hands up and down my goosebump covered arms.

"No," I say honestly. I can't resist the temptation to make him a little more scared. It is always entertaining to me to watch people freak out.

"Babe!" he says, his grip on my hand getting tighter as we hear a growling noise.

"It's probably just a squirrel," I repeat myself, this time trying to convince myself as well.

"Squirrels don't growl like that," he states with a heavy sigh. As much as I hate to admit it, he's right... and it's starting to freak me out too.

"Maybe we shouldn't be out here... it has to be like midnight by now," Bentley says, looking at me with pleading eyes.

"You *know* we're not supposto be out here," I tease, thinking of earlier that night when we sneaked out of our houses to meet here.

"Yeah, but I mean, maybe we're *really* not supposed to be out here. Something feels wrong."

"Since when do you have a sixth sense?"

"You know what I mean, Melissa, I know you feel it too. I know you're wigged, weather you admit it or not."

Sometimes I hate that he knows me so well. I nod, but the thought of walking home alone makes my stomach knot up. I bite my lip and my eyes shift around my surroundings. He's watching. I can feel his gaze. I don't want to go home alone because he will follow me. He will talk to me.

"What's wrong?" Bentley asked.

"I'm just turned on, that's all," I lie, crossing my fingers so it doesn't really count. Besides, I am wet. We were making out for quite the long while.

"You're scared to walk home, aren't you?" he asks.

"Maybe," I admit.

"Mel,"

"Okay, I am. What's that mean?"

"Absolutely nothing, I'm scared too." I jump as my peripheral vision catches something but, when I jerk my head, I see nothing. Why does he have to be so damn creepy? He'd be perfect if he wasn't.

"Well what do we do, we can't exactly both walk each other home. And if we're caught by our parents we'll be dead."

"Maybe not the same kind of dead we'll be if we stay," Bentley says. Stating reality causes a solid line of fear to shoot through my head. The fear is making my adrenaline rush and it feels good soaring through my veins. I lay my head back and smile, taking in a cool breath of the night air.

"It's not funny, Mel," Bentley warns. I don't think Bentley gets the same rush off fear that I do. I wonder for a second if I am normal. Maybe my mind is corrupt from all the horror books that I read. I wouldn't put it past myself. Sometimes, I have some awfully weird and horrid thoughts inside my head. They never last for long, and I don't mean the half of them, but I have them nevertheless.

Thoughts of killing people… saying hurtful things… inflicting severe emotional pain. Thoughts of hurting other people – thoughts I would never actually do in reality.

"Don't you love the way it feels?" I ask, my hands running up and down the damp grass beneath me.

"The way what feels?" Bentley asks, lying down next to me.

"Adrenaline... fear... being afraid. It makes your head go funny and your stomach twist into a knot making you just wanna squirm, and your heart starts beating fast and you can't stop it. You're scared, but not scared enough to actually start screaming. It's purely indescribable," I moan as the feeling surrounds me, drowns me.

"Sometimes you scare me, you know that?" He chuckles to himself in a nervous way. I roll on my side and look at him longingly, knowing what I have to do. It feels so right, so natural; it will give me the best rush of all. It will feel ten times as amazing as how I feel now. I take in a deep breath and hold it. Bentley scoots toward me again, wrapping his arms around me.

My hands feel their way up and down his muscular arms. He pulls me closer and my hands wander behind him. I press myself against him, reaching as far as I can with my arms. I feel around the damp grass and slide my hand under the blanket we lay on. That is where I keep it... just in case... just in case I'm up to it. Just in case I actually decide to do it. Earlier that night, I thought I wouldn't be able to... I didn't think I would be wrong... I didn't think I'd actually go through with it... My stomach gets all knotted up as I think about doing it. But the mere thought of how it will make me feel is enough to set my mind at ease. I know he'll never see it coming. I know he'll be surprised. I know I have to do it. It's the only thing to do.

Two Weeks Earlier...

"I can't believe the week's gone by so fast," Bentley said,

sliding his arm around me.

"What's so special about this past week?" I asked, raising my eyebrows. The bitter fall wind snapped through the air, picking up leafs and hurling them at my bare legs. I'd obviously picked the wrong day to wear a mini-skirt. *Prick, prick, prick,* they whisked against my skin causing little red bumps all down my legs. I shivered and brushed my legs. Bentley unzipped his hoodie and wrapped it around me. I squeezed it tightly and mumbled a thank you. I turned my head to kiss him, but he smiled and pulled away. A childish fire burned in his eyes.

"If you wanna kiss me, you'll have to catch me first," he said, jumping up on the fence railing beside us. I ran along beside it as he jumped and danced from post to post. It was too high to catch him. I knew what I had to do. I stopped suddenly and hoisted myself up on fence line. I tried not to look down, and at first I didn't; but, like most people, I just couldn't resist the urge. I looked down and at first I thought I was going to pass out, I felt so high up. After a few seconds I started to smile, the foreboding feeling was gone and had been replaced with a most excellent adrenaline rush. I could feel my entire body soaking in the cool air. I felt the need to run, jump, and dance across the fence, hopping from post to post as I went. I was alive… I felt alive… I loved that feeling. It was the best feeling in the world. Bentley looked back behind him, watching me smile and attempt to keep my balance.

"I dare ya to keep up, Mel," he said. I watched a cocky half-smile craw across his face right before he turned back around and broke into a run, leaping from post to post.

My palms started to sweat, and I could feel my lungs get hot. My head told me to climb down, but soon the adrenaline in my body made me act differently. I started running as fast as Bentley. My head spun and the thought that I could fall and break a limb at any moment was enough to keep my heart racing and my pores wide open, absorbing the open air around me. I was so close to Bentley I could almost tag him and get my kiss.

"Come on, Star, come on girl!" I called to our puppy, who was struggling to keep up. Her ears fell flat against her face as she bullied her way through the wind. I taunted her, running faster as

Bentley sped up as much as he could.

Off in the distance I heard a scuffling noise followed by barking. With that, Star took off into the woods, barking. I shook my head at the crazy pup. She'd be back. She always came back.

I was so close to Bentley when we heard it. A noise that made both of us stop short in our tracks. A noise that makes Bentley jump off the fence and back onto the road. A noise that sent my heart into a stand-still and fear come over my entire body. And not the kind of fear that was fun, the kind with a good adrenaline rush. No, what I felt was Real Fear. I jumped off the fence and stared into the woods.

"Star! Star!" I screamed, my eyes widened and my mind sped rapidly without much sense going through it. I could hear her yelping and screeching. What had she gotten into? Her wining turned into ringing in my ears and I could barely hear Bentley calling her name. Everything was so far away. All I could think of was: *dog fight.* I could hear other dogs barking off in the distance again. What had they done to my puppy? She was so small, so little at only 8 months. My heart sank into my chest when the wining stopped. I took a deep breath. That's when I became aware of my surroundings; Bentley had jumped the fence and was half-way into the woods, calling Star's name. He looked back at me.

"There's no way I can get farther than this, they're all thorny bushes," he explained. His eyes were glossy, ready to cry, and his eyebrows scrunched up to his face. I had to sit down. What had happened? Did my puppy just get killed? No Star! Not my Star! I couldn't deal with that, not now, not for a very long time. She was just a little puppy. Why had she gone into the woods anyways? Why Star, why?

Bentley walked back up through the woods and put his arm around me. I sank down to the ground. My mind was blank for a long time. I didn't know what to think. I didn't know how to feel. I didn't know anything at that moment. I didn't know for sure that she was dead... did I? I mean, I hadn't seen her dead body, so how could she be dead? The thought of her dead body was what brought me back with a shudder. How long had I been sitting there? What time was it? I looked around, nothing much seemed different.

"Are you okay?" Bentley asked me, his hand running up and down the side of my arm. His cheek brushed up against mine and a wave of comfort overcame me, but it wasn't enough.

"You killed her!" I exclaimed. Even as I was speaking, I wasn't conscious of the words that came out until after it was already too late. What on earth caused me to say that? I wasn't mad at Bentley and I certainly didn't blame him for Star's death. Why would I say such things? I felt my cheeks go hot and my ears start to burn when I saw the look in Bentley's eyes.

"I didn't mean-" but he wouldn't let me finish.

"How could you say that?" he asked, almost knocking me down when he stood up. I hadn't realized how much I'd been leaning against him.

"I'm sorry," I said, tears filling my eyes. I didn't mean to say that. I didn't even know why I had.

"I loved her just as much as you, Mel; she was *our* puppy, even if she lived with you." Guilt squirmed in my insides like worms in a decaying body, but I wouldn't let it out. My eyes dried up and I swallowed hard.

"I know. I'm sorry. I was just upset. I didn't mean it," I promised, taking a deep breath as I spoke each short sentence slowly. *It's all his fault,* a voice inside my head said... it sounded like me... but different. Like my subconscious, or an inner evil tugging at me to let it free. My stomach knotted again and I shook the voice from my mind. Bentley nodded and pulled me in for a hug. I instantly felt calm and just wanted to be in my bedroom with him, cuddling.

"Will you take me home?" I asked, realizing that his shirt was getting soaked due to my tears. Bentley nodded and I felt his arms slide under my knees as he swooped me up, carrying me down the road back to my house.

Chapter Two
The Man in the Dream

I laid in bed later that night, crying, wishing it'd all been a dream. *It was Bentley's fault,* the voice - my voice inside my head – said.... *Bentley's the one who climbed up on the fence first... Bentley's the one who started running... Bentley's the one who made you chase him... Bentley's the reason Star was running... Bentley... Bentley... Bentley.*

I couldn't stop it no matter how hard I tried. I squeezed my eyes shut, pulled the pillow over my head and clasped my hands over my ears... but it didn't stop. It wouldn't stop. It was part of me... or was it entirely me? No it couldn't have been all me! I would never think that way about Bentley. Star is the one who ran off. If anything, it was the other dog's fault for barking and yanking Star's attention away from me.

You can't lie to yourself, my voice said, then finally stopped. Only the sound of my sobs filled the room. Eventually, they dwindled and the room was silent. I breathed in as deep as I could. I listened to the sweet sound of silence and allowed my shoulders to relax, slowly drifting off to sleep.................................

I gasped for air, my body stiffening. One breath and I quit breathing, lying silently still in my bed. I was hot... my lungs felt like there were bricks lying atop them. It wasn't an unfamiliar feeling; it happened every time I had The Dream. I could remember having The Dream way back when I was five. The only thing I remembered, I cherished forever in secret.

I sat up in my bed, peeling the sweat-soaked sheets off my bare skin. My feet hit the cold hardwood floor. I scrunched up my toes, wishing my slippers were nearby. The cool air washed over my body and I felt my nipples become erect. I reached for the light switch, my hand running along the wall, my heart racing with the thought that *he* might be here... watching me. My worry was foolish, for when I turned on the light, I was alone in my bedroom.

I let out a sigh of relief and shook my head at my childish notions. I ran my hands along my chilly arms, feeling the warm tingles all down my spine. I reached for my fluffy red rope hanging on my desk chair, pulling it tightly around my body, snuggling into it. I looked around my room; the walls were covered with taped on sketches I'd drawn. I drew anything that popped into my head, ranging from fairies, to roses, circus ringleaders, vampires, dusty planes, sunny fields.

The clock blinked 12:00, on and off... on and off... red numbers glowing in the dimly lit room; I'd only turned on my reading lamp. The power must have gone out. I searched around for my wristwatch, trying to remember where I'd taken it off before I went to sleep. Eventually, I found it sitting atop my dresser. It read 4:58. I pulled up the blinds to reveal the new-moon night, darkest before dawn, full of pitch-black nothingness. Shivering, I pulled the blinds back down again and sat at my desk.

There would be no going back to sleep tonight... there never was after The Dream. I could see him so clearly... the only thing I remember from any of the dreams was the man who frequented them. I pulled out my sketchbook with the finest paper inside, my black coal pencils, my very best eraser, and started with a line. That's all it took, a simple line, and then the picture gained control of itself... twisting and turning, deviously winding through the page, forming the man in my mind... The Man in the Dream.

When I paused to look at it he smiled back at me, his eyes glowing with contempt... I wasn't finished, I had to perfect it... perfect him... capture him in the way that he so richly deserved. So, I set the piece of paper back on the desk, picked up the eraser, and erased, then drew new lines, his pure essence seeping into the page.

This time when I finished, it was perfect... my best sketch yet. I opened my desk drawer and pulled out a folder from under the false bottom of the drawer, inside the secret compartment that would only open if one applied the right amount of pressure. It was hidden by a stack of other notebooks and folders. It slipped from my hands and pictures of The Man from The Dream dropped onto the floor. There must have been at least one-hundred that I'd drawn over the years. After all, I'd had so many dreams of him... felt so many compulsions to sketch him, and each new one only got better and better.

I never showed them to anybody or spoke of him at all. He was mine, all mine, and only mine. No one was to know of him... no one was to even have the slightest clue about him. That's why I kept his portraits in my desk, tucked away, hidden, where no one could possibly find them. He didn't mind. He didn't want anyone to know about him. He didn't care about anything or anyone else. All he wanted… was me.

I sat there, in the middle of my room, my bare legs pressing against the cold floor, looking at the sketches of him, admiring them. I wondered how I had captured such a mysterious man in my mind. I wondered what had caused me to dream of him in the first place. I wondered how I could love him – a figment of my imagination – more than my boyfriend of three solid years. I wondered a lot of things I probably shouldn't.

I tried to write stories about him, but they never came out right. His stories only existed in my mind, and in my mind they would stay. I could only sketch him... it was part of his beauty... his inner beauty. I gently caressed my fingers down the side of his cheek in one of my pictures, wishing I could feel what His skin was like. I drew it so smooth, so milky, and so flawless. I gazed into his eyes, an emerald green, so intense they could trap you inside for hours, and you wouldn't even know you were gone.

When I heard my mother's footsteps on my bedroom ceiling, I quickly slipped the last sketch inside the folder, and gently placed it back in my desk. I picked up my wristwatch and slipped it on. 9:30... how had the time passed so quickly? Opening my dresser drawer, I pulled out a pair of tough camo jeans and a black t-shirt. I allowed my robe to fall to the floor and pulled on my clothes for the day, ran my fingers through my hair a couple times, and headed up the stairs.

"You're up early for a Saturday," my mother stated as she

spotted me heading to the kitchen to grab a mug of coffee.

"I couldn't sleep," I replied, taking a sip of coffee. I knew it was too hot to drink, but I jumped anyways. I gingerly touched my finger to my lip where it slightly tingled.

"I'm sorry about Star," my mother said solemnly as I sat down next to her at the breakfast table. "But, you don't know for sure that she's dead. I mean, you never actually saw-"

"Yeah, I know. I should have done something... the sound-"

"Melissa, please don't blame yourself."

I don't, mom, I blame Bentley. I shook the thought from my head. It was pointless to blame Bentley... there was no way I could honestly think it was his fault. *But there is a way... there must be, because you **do** think that.*

"I won't," I promised, doing my best to ignore the voice.

"Good."

"I'm going to go look for her," I said, taking a sip of my now reasonably hot coffee.

"I'm not so sure-"

"Mom, it's something I have to do."

"I just don't-"

"Want me to find her dead? Yeah, I know. Trust me, neither do I. But, I have to go look," I said definitively.

"I understand," my mother said, picking up the daily paper, turning to the back page to solve the crossword puzzle.

I finished my coffee, ate a bowl of frosted mini wheats, and stood up from the table.

"Melissa," my mother started. I turned to look at her. "Be safe," she finished. I got the feeling that that wasn't exactly what she was going to say at first, but I didn't press the issue.

I slipped on my leather jacket and my black combat boots and headed out the door.

The misty morning was overcast. The ground was wet, making the leafs slippery. I walked slowly and carefully down the road, running my hand along the rail that Bentley and I had run on yesterday. I found the spot where Star had run out into the woods, and I began walking down the very steep mountainside. I walked at an angle so I wouldn't slip and tumble down the hill, an extra hard feat seeing as how the ground was slippery. The thicket was hard to get past at first, and my hair got caught up several times. But, after suffering through for a few minutes, the thicket started to clear. Why hadn't I just womaned-up and endured this yesterday?

I walked for what felt like hours, calling Star's name, hoping, praying, that she would run up to me, get her muddy paws all over my clothes, lick my face, and never leave my sight again. The sun refused to shine, and with every branch I gripped onto to stabilize myself, the more soaked I got from the rain-droplets sitting in the tree's leafs.

I wandered until I was lost, but I didn't even care. All I wanted was to find Star... all I wanted was to see her. I needed to see her... she was my Star! The dark clouds overhead threatened a torrential downpour, and I started to wonder which way was home, or where I would seek shelter if it did start to rain. This time of year it was far too easy to get hypothermia if one was out in the damp woods for too long... besides, I was already wet and had no means to easily make a fire.

I grabbed onto a thick tree branch, swinging myself under... only I swung too hard and too fast. My grip on the branch slipped, and my feet flew out from under me. My ass smacked the ground, sending a shooting pain from my tailbone to my neck. I started to slide down the mountainside, gaining speed rapidly. My hands flailed out to my side, trying desperately to stop myself... or at least slow down. My head flew back and smacked a tree stump to my side as I tried to turn around to grab a nearby branch... obviously unsuccessfully. My hand shot to my head and my feet whacked into a giant log, bringing me to a sudden halt. I rubbed my head where it'd hit and then looked at my hand, expecting to see blood. There wasn't any.

I stood up and looked around. My vision was blurry; the tears in my eyes caused by the severe pain in my head... and the fact that I wanted to cry over Star didn't help. I took a deep breath and looked around, drying my eyes with the edge of my sleeve.

"Well, fancy meeting you here," a voice came from behind me. I whirled around, turning to see Him. At first, I didn't believe it... maybe I'd whacked my head *too* hard. He stood there, a wry half-smile covering the lower half of his high cheeks. His sleek black hair barely whisked the tops of his wide shoulders. His black eyeliner made his bright green eyes pop, capturing me inside them. I didn't want to look away... they consumed me.

"Where did you come from? Who are you? What are you doing here?" I asked. The first question started off timid, the next one I was conscious of what I was saying, and the third I panicked. This was Him... it was really Him... it was the picture perfect version of The Man in My Dream. He was everything I'd tried to capture in my sketches... everything I wanted... he looked perfect, so real, so alive... he was... he was alive! He was standing right in front of me... or was that even possible? This couldn't be happening. *Why not? You really thought we'd never meet?* A voice that sounded like his asked from inside my head. I took in another deep breath... I was getting tired of hearing voices in my head, and it was all the more concerning when it wasn't my own.

"Me? What are you doing here? After all, these are *my* woods," he said with a slight chuckle and a raise of his eyebrow. I didn't answer; I just stood there, gawking at him. He quickly moved his head to the side, biting his lip, lowering his chin to his chest.

"Your woods?" I asked... no one could own the woods? Could they? I mean, they were woods. He smiled proudly, and I shyly touched my cheek to my shoulder. He then leaned his body to the right, tilting his head so he could see into my eyes. Having him look into my eyes made my cheeks go hot and the blood in my ears start to pound out a rhythm a rock band could use. He smiled at me as I moved my head up so I was standing tall. I arched my shoulders back and my breasts forward, held my chin high and stood strong. I needed to be aware of myself... there was no way this was actually happening.

"What's your name?" I asked. It was the only *normal* question I could think to ask.

"Elijah," he replied smoothly, waving his hand in front of him, introducing himself. Elijah. It was perfect. It was his name, I could tell. It was exactly what his name should have been... the fact that I hadn't thought of it when trying to brainstorm his name seemed ludicrous!

"I'm here to help you," he said smoothly, walking toward me with a slight smile. My feet shuffled backwards, and Elijah stopped walking.

"What's the matter? I don't bite," Elijah said, leaning up against a tree, looking down at his right hand. He wore three rather large rings. One was black and red, the other was all black, and one was all red. I looked at his left hand; he wore the same rings on that hand as well.

"Help me with what?" I asked, inching towards him. I wanted to be closer to him; I wanted to touch him... I wanted to know he was real.

"You are lost, are you not?" he asked, waving his hand and then bringing it up to gingerly touch his chin.

"Um," I stuttered, not knowing what to say. Elijah offered a comforting smile... I tried to return it, but I was too busy trying to figure him out to fully smile.

"Don't worry. Like I said, these are my woods."

"You don't-"

"Ah, but I do," Elijah reassured without letting me finish. I felt my eyebrows scrunch together, and then, noticing Elijah's never-fading smile, my face relaxed. I was safe with him here. He was safety.

"So, what is a pretty little thing like you doing out here anyways? Didn't anyone ever tell you there are demons in these woods?" At the mention of demons, my stomach started to knot. The safe feeling suddenly vanished, and the woods seemed to become darker.

"Demons?" I asked.

"Ahh, so your mother never told you. That explains a lot," Elijah said, more to himself than me. What was he talking about? *Deep down, you know what he is talking about, Mel,* the voice inside my head said, an invisible force cajoling me toward him. He shined through the darkness, leading the way. He broke the darkness; he was safety in these demon filled woods. He was the savior and I followed him... and I followed him.

"So?"

"So what?"

"So are you going to tell me what you are doing out

here?"

"Oh, right," I said, pausing. I didn't want to say... I didn't want to admit that my dog was most likely dead. "I was looking for my dog," I realized these words were just gushing out of my mouth... I wasn't thinking about what I was saying... I just spoke... and it felt safe to talk to him, like I should... like... like he could help somehow.

"Your dog?"

"She's probably dead... I heard-"

"You can't hear something die," he interrupted, changing directions and heading back to where we'd met.

"Well-"

"Well nothing, Mel," Elijah said smoothly, turning to face me... I wanted to touch him so badly... I wanted to feel he was real more than anything in the entire world. *Wait a second,* I thought to myself, *did he call me Mel?... he did... didn't he?* I didn't remember telling him my name... had I? I must have. There's no way he could possibly know otherwise.

"What do you believe?" he asked, jerking me back into reality.

"Believe?" I asked.

"About death," he elaborated, nearing me. We were inches away and all I wanted was to brush my hand against his cheek.

"It's death," I replied absentmindedly. I was lost in his eyes again... consumed by the world of chaos inside of them.

"Which is?"

"Gone," I whispered.

"So when you die, you're gone forever?" he whispered back. I nodded. He smiled softly, baring no teeth, as if to say he knew something I didn't.

As I reached out to touch his face, unaware of my body language, he turned away from me and walked forth. I took in a sudden breath, realizing that I hadn't been breathing for the past minute or so when I had peered into his emerald green eyes.

"Why did you switch directions?" I asked, stepping over sticks and logs, watching my footing on the slick leafs.

"Because I'm not taking you home," he said.

"What? But I'm lost! You can't jus-"

"Do you want to find your dog or not?" he asked, spinning on his heels to face me, his palms facing outward in question.

"Yeah, thanks," I muttered. He nodded and we continued trekking through the woods until I saw her... Star. She laid there, in a collapsed clump. Dogs weren't supposed to look like that... not even when they were dead. Tufts of fur were missing, and spots of blood made what was left of her mangled fur hard and pointy. Two of her teeth lay on the ground beside her. One of her eyes was swollen shut; the other looked out into the woods, hopeful.

I felt the tears come to my eyes and I couldn't hold them back. Her eye peered into mine, filling me with guilt. I hadn't come quickly enough... I should have come yesterday... if I had, I would have saved her.

I ran over to her, dropping on my knees as soon as I reached her. I touched her snout, it was cold and dry... the only dry thing in these woods. I felt like I'd swallowed a rock. Unable to breathe easily, I gave up and held my breath, biting my lip as tears stained my cheeks. The cool autumn breeze whipped around me, stinging my bones, and freezing the salty water that escaped my stinging eyes. My nose dripped; I used my index finger to wipe it.

I felt Elijah's hand on my shoulder. A surge of energy filled me. I could breathe again, I was warm again. He was real. He was safety. He was mine. I was his. He was real... he was really real. I could feel him... not only could I feel him, but I could feel his power, his essence. He was everything I dreamt he would be... a million times better than any sketch.

After a while, I gained control of myself and stopped crying.

"She's gone," I said, accepting it. *Death doesn't always mean gone...* the voice inside my head said. It sounded like Elijah.

"I need to go home," I said, scooping up Star in my arms, cradling her like a baby. I held her close to my chest, as if my body heat would warm her, wherever she was.

"Follow me," Elijah said, standing and walking to his left. I followed him, and five minutes later, we were by the edge of the woods where Star had been so full of life the day before.

"I believe you know the way from here," Elijah stated, turning back to face the woods.

"Wait!" I called out. He stopped, but didn't turn around to face me. "Thank you," I said softly. He began to walk forward again. I wanted to call out to him once more, to ask when we could meet again, but I didn't... and the moment he was out of sight, I regretted it.

".... Ashes to ashes, dust to dust, Amen," my mother recited. I threw a handful of daffodils, my favorite flower, on top of Star, who laid two feet under, in as much of a natural, comfortable, position that I could manage. My nose was red, my eyes were puffy, and the tears wouldn't come anymore... I'd cried as much as humanly possible that day.

My mother rested a hand on my shoulder as I shoveled the dirt in the grave. It felt so wrong to bury her... to watch the dirt slowly cover her. It was morbid... disturbing... wrong in every way. I could barely stand to do it.

"You want some help?" my mom sweetly asked, resting a hand on my shoulder. I shook my head, incapable of words.

"I understand. I'll be inside... some hot cocoa will be ready when you come in." She walked inside.

I missed my father... he should be here... this was his job, not mine, and not mom's. He was never here to do any of his jobs... he left us... or mom left him... I wasn't sure which. Mom didn't like to talk about it. Either way, I resented him for never being there, never trying to contact me in any way. He wasn't dead, mom told me that much. I'd never met him... I'd never seen him... he wasn't anywhere near my mother when she gave birth to me... and my mother never talked about him, no matter how hard I tried to get her to.

After I finished, I couldn't walk away. I laid down on top of the fresh grave, feeling the cool dirt against my skin. I wanted so much to be close to her right now... I wanted so much to hold her, to feel her wet tongue licking my face, to hear her bark... I wanted to see her again.

*You miss **him** almost as much as you miss **her**...* the voice in my head spoke softly, referencing Elijah.

After another long cry, I guess I hadn't been done as I previously thought; I gathered my strength and walked inside. The smell of sugar cookies and chocolate filled the house, and I felt my lips attempt a smile.

"Why don't you go take a hot shower?" my mom suggested, smiling sympathetically at me.

"Okay," I replied, walking toward the bathroom.

I felt better after the shower. I ate some cookies, drank some cocoa, and watched a few sitcoms with my mom. My eyes were no longer swollen, and my nose was no longer red, but my heart continued to ache for two reasons... Elijah and Star.

Before I went to bed that night, my mom stopped me.

"Mel," she said. I turned to face her.

"Yeah?"

"Are you okay?"

"Mom, my dog just died," I said, raising my eyebrows.

"I know. And I know that's hard... but something about you... just... something seems different," she stated. I stood there, not knowing what to say.

"Did something happen in the woods today?" she asked. "Anything unusual?"

I paused, thinking.

"No," I replied slowly, shaking my head.

"You sure?"

"Ye-" but before I could get out my whole one-word answer, she interrupted me.

"Because you can tell me... I understand more than you probably think I will." I was confused by this.

"Mom," I said, reaching out to her and touching her cheek. "I'm okay," I promised. She nodded, wrapping her arms around me tightly in a very long, very intense, very motherly and protective embrace.

*   *   *

I sketched him again that night. Only, this time, he was perfect... more perfect than all the rest, filling me with a new sense of awareness. I didn't want to sketch him again... ever. This one was perfect, giving him full marks... I captured him unlike ever before, pleasing him in my mind.

I was tired afterward, more than usual. I fell asleep, letting him - *bark* - consume my subconscious... my dream state. He filled me, he – *bark* - controlled me, he controlled everything inside of me, outside of me, - *bark* - around me... he controlled the world. His power – *bark* - was overwhelming, but comforting at the same time. It was strong, - *bark bark* - protective, better than anything I'd ever felt or witnessed before. The wind swirled – *bark* - around him, he commanded it to thunder and controlled the lightening, the sky swirled purple. There was a raging fire in the background, but it was okay... he had it under control. When he smiled, the light – *bark* - in the world peered through, making everything white... he slowly faded into – *bark bark bark bark* - the background... the light was too blinding... I couldn't see anything... just white.

Suddenly, I saw his face, his lips curling into a smile. His pearly white teeth now held all the white light, slowly sucking it away.

"You're welcome," he said softly but strongly.

Bark bark bark bark bark bark

My eyes opened with a start and I breathed in a harshly cold breath of air. I was covered in sweat, the sheets stuck to me.

BARK!

It was real... the bark was real. I sat straight up in my bed; the dog's muddy paws appeared in front of me. I looked up to see Star, standing strong, wagging her tail... her tongue hanging out of her mouth. She was panting, pawing at me, looking for a reaction.

This was real... This was NOT a dream. This was real... I knew it... I could feel it... I could feel his presence... and I could see Star. This was real.

Chapter Three
Buried

"*So, she came back?*" Bentley's muffled voice asked from the other end of the phone.

"No. I buried her. My mom saw me. And now she's back. She didn't just come back," I said slowly, pausing a lot between my words.

"And where's your mom now?" he asked. My skin started to crawl and I felt my fists clench. How dare he not actually believe me! I wasn't crazy. He should know that.

"At work," I said calmly, trying to control my temper. My emotions were all high-strung due to Star's appearance; it was all I could do to keep myself from crying.

"I'm coming over. Don't take this the wrong way, Mel, but you don't sound stable right now." Don't take it the wrong way? He thought I was crazy! He was coming over to see Star for himself because he didn't believe me. He was supposed to be my boyfriend, the love of my life. He was supposed to trust me no matter what... but he didn't. But, it didn't really matter. He would see soon enough. I couldn't wait to see the look on his face when he saw Star, sitting here, wagging her tail.

"I'll be here," I said quietly before hanging up the phone.

I turned around to see Star sitting there, looking up at me. Her tail wagged back and forth, her big blue eyes innocently looking at me. She pawed at her muddy, mangled fur and wined a little bit.

"You need a bath, girl," I said. I never thought I would be so excited to give my dog a bath... before I thought of it as a chore, whereas now I realized it was a privilege. I was so happy she was here with me. No one was going to take her from me again... no one. *Bentley will try...* the voice in my head warned. I shook it off; nothing was going to get me down or control me or my thoughts.

"Come on," I said, patting my leg. She jumped up and followed me into the bathroom. I turned on the light, only for it to blow out. Star whimpered, and hid under the sink, backing into the darkness of the cabinet. Her muddy fur rubbed all over my fresh and clean towels. I took in a deep breath, trying not to be annoyed.

"Come here, Star, it's okay," I said. She'd never been scared of the dark before... I didn't know what had gotten into her.

C

    R

        A

            S

                H

                    !

A high-pitched scream escaped my lips, as I jumped back, whacking my ankle on the side of the tub. I stumbled backwards, my arms flailing behind me, attempting to catch myself. *Clank, clink, shatter*... the sound of my mother's crystal soap dish. *Slash*... the sound of my mother's crystal soap dish running down my arm, turning my entire forearm red.

I felt my stomach start to churn, and my head began to feel distanced from the rest of my body. I closed my eyes tightly and took a deep breath. It wasn't the pain... it didn't even hurt that badly. It was the blood... I couldn't stand the blood.

I could feel Star's warm breath panting next to me, her tongue slowly licking my wound. I wanted to pull it away, but I was beginning to lose all feeling and consciousness. The world around me dimmed, only Star remained in my sights. Little black dots began to corrode her, drifting in and out until all I knew was a world of pitch-black... a world of numbness... a world that was known as the subconscious... the unconscious... I drifted away... away... away... nothingness surrounded me with warm and welcome arms.

*   *   *

"Come here, Melissa," he spoke softer than I was used to. I could barely recognize him. He'd lost a significant amount of weight, and his arms had purple bruises on them from the nurses sticking him with different needles, tubes, and IVs. His hair had thinned and he'd shaved his beard. Eight-year-old me was terrified to see him like this... My mother had warned me that he would look weak, but I never imagined he would look like this.

"I love you," was all I could think to say... I wanted him to know how much I loved him. He smiled at me with his eyes as he inhaled slowly, the oxygen machine making a whirring noise as he breathed. As I walked toward my Granddad, he reached his arm out to me. I wanted to speak to him, to tell him everything that was going through my mind, and at the same time I wanted to keep myself hidden... it was time to distance myself from him.

I couldn't speak freely with that man standing in the corner, watching me. He stood straight, his face emotionless, his hands holding each other behind his back. He didn't blink, he just watched, waiting... waiting for something... but what, and why?

I directed my attention back to my Granddad, whose eyes were now watery. We had the same eyes... though mine didn't hold back tears as well as his.

"I want you to know that I've really enjoyed you being around, kiddo," he said, resting his hand on my shoulder. I nodded my head because I didn't know what to say. "You and I, we share a real special connection." The oxygen machine sucked in again as he breathed and slowly let it out. "I'm real glad I got a granddaughter as great as you, Mel." It was the first time anybody had called me "Mel" before. I smiled; I liked the nickname. "I love you, sweetheart, I really, really do."

"I love you... too," I said, sniffling in-between.

The man in the corner walked toward my Granddad, his eyes remaining on me. I watched him, dread filling my entire body as his steps got closer and closer. He bent over my Granddad, looking straight into his eyes. A red cross shook in the man's hands, a sinisterly smile overtook his face as emotion left my Granddads.

"Dad?" I heard my mom ask. There was no response.

"Daddy?" she asked again. I could feel the barriers of my

heart start to tremble, and my eyes became filled with tears.

There was a warm hand on my shoulder, soothing my entire body. As I looked behind me, I saw who was touching me... the man who had looked my Granddad in the eyes as he died.

"You can see me, can't you?" he asked. I nodded, incapable of words.

"You can feel me." This time it was a statement. I nodded once more, unsure what else I should do.

"You love me," he said in almost a demanding tone. I nodded again, this time not of my own volition. But as soon as I nodded, I felt it. The love. It was real.

"Elijah!" I gasped, coming back to reality. The man at my Granddad's death was Elijah... How had I not made the connection? How could I have forgotten the memory of my Granddad's death until now? Star licked my face, her tail wagging. The blood on my arm was now sticky... the bleeding had slowed. I wondered how long I'd been out. I walked upstairs to grab the peroxide from under the kitchen sink; Star followed me, trotting along beside me, her eyes looking around the room.

I poured the peroxide on the gash, biting the inside of my cheek as it stung my entire arm. I watched bubbles form and overflow. I dabbed the wound with a paper towel; it wasn't that bad. It barely even broke the skin... it had just bled a lot. I was just a big baby. That was all.

You know it was worse before you conked out... something weird is going on, Mel, and I'm part of it... Elijah's voice echoed in my head.

"Well, aren't you a sight for sore eyes," I spun around. The voice didn't belong to Bentley. I saw no one.

"Hello?" I called out.

"You're all cold and clammy, sweaty from going under," Elijah's voice jested. I looked around, unable to tell where it was coming from. I looked at Star, she would protect me, but she looked innocent and unaware that there was even another voice.

"This isn't funny," I stated strongly. There was only

silence as a reply.

I shook my head, trying to erase the memory. I glanced at a clock, only to realize I hadn't even paid attention to the time when I awoke. Bentley wasn't here yet, so that meant I couldn't have been out too terribly long. Bentley lived three hours away, so now there was no telling when he would be here.

"Come on, Star, let's go get cleaned up," I said, bending down to pet her. I then lifted her into my arms and carried her back into the bathroom.

I undressed slowly, being aware of my injured arm. It took three minutes to get my shirt off, but in the end it was worth it... pain free. My pants slid off without any troubles, the hot water emitting from the shower causing the mirror to fog up. My reflection tapered away... drifting into a whole different world inside the long mirror... my view clouded by steam... my world jaded by heat, darkness, and mystery.

The hot water stung my arm at first, but then slowly began to sooth it. Star darted in and out from under my feet... she loved the water, she always had. My mind played tricks on me as I poured the red shampoo in the palm of my hand, mistaking it for blood. I dropped the bottle, clanking against the tub. Thankfully, it didn't break... I'd broken enough things for one day. Realizing it was only shampoo, I took in a deep breath and bent down to pick up the leaking container.

I lathered up my hair before lathering up Star. She sat there so still, so happy, like a perfect girl. I ran my fingers through her thick fur, squeezing the dirt from it. I didn't want to think about where that dirt had come from... I wanted to forget I'd ever buried her... I wanted to forget that it was near impossible that she dug herself out.

Nothing is impossible, Mel... Elijah's cheery voice rang inside my head. I wanted to forget that I was hearing voices in my head... but, at the moment, none of that seemed possible to forget.

I did this for you, Mel. You should be happy... I want you to be happy. Elijah said, and I could almost feel his hands caressing my body.

The shower curtain flew open... a shrill scream escaped my lips as I jumped up and wrapped my arms around my breasts, concealing them from view.

"Got room in there for one more?" Bentley asked, a wry smile creeping across his face.

"What the fuck, Bentley? That's not cool! Get out of here now!" I screamed, pulling the curtain closed again.

"God, Mel, get a sense of humor."

"It's an invasion of privacy, dumb ass," I stated, rinsing the conditioner out of my hair quickly. Star was all clean, but she didn't want to get out, she loved pouncing around in the water.

"It's nothin' I ain't seen before, chill out," Bentley argued.

"Well, you still scared me half-to-death, you stupid jerk-off! This, by the way, is what you'll be doing later today because I, sure as Hell, am not going to take care of you!" I shut off the water and reached up for my towel... which was no longer there.

"I think you're taking this a little too hard."

"Give. Me. My. Towel," I demanded, grinding my teeth.

"Come out and get it," Bentley taunted.

"You're an ass!" I exclaimed, shutting my eyes as Star shook herself dry, flinging the water onto me. "This hasn't exactly been the most calming day for me! My dog comes back from the dead, I can't get the picture of this guy I met in the woods out of my head, I cut my arm on my mother's favorite soap dish that I broke, and—"

"You met a guy in the woods yesterday?"

"Goddamn it! Bentley! Is that all you take away from that? Are you so insecure and jealous that you're really worried I would cheat on you with some creep in the woods?! Don't you even care about my arm! Or that my dog *came back to life?*" I screamed, throwing open the shower curtain and snatching the towel away from him. I wrapped it around my body, running my fingers through my hair to keep it out of my face.

"Your arm looks fine to me... and where exactly is Star?" I looked down at my arm... the cut had healed completely... there was barely a red mark that would be hard-pressed to pass as a scratch.

"Well, I've always been a fast healer," I said. It wasn't a complete lie. When I was five, I thought I'd for sure broken my arm, but the doctor said it'd just been a bad sprain... it felt fine within five days. I'd never been sick for longer than twelve hours, and when I cut myself it was always very shallow and healed quicker than usual... but, I couldn't lie to myself, this was unusual... even for me.

"And she's in the tub," I said, walking over to the mirror, my hand circling on it, making a clear spot so I could see myself. I gripped my hair in my palms, the excess water dripping out, trailing down my shoulders and soaking into the towel that rested just above my breasts.

"I jus-" my words were cut short by a low growling. I felt a sick feeling in my stomach; I knew what was coming.

"Bentley, don't!" I exclaimed, but it was too late. Star's growl had turned into a bark. I whipped around, my hair slashing to my right side, whacking the mirror with a shattering noise. Bentley was trying his best to detain Star, who was barking, clawing, and gnashing her teeth.

"Don't hurt her, she's scared!" I yelled at Bentley as he wrapped his hands around Star's neck. I held my breath, unable to think, unable to move, unable to do anything but watch.

Star jerked her neck to the side, her jaw clenching down on Bentley's wrist. Bentley's scream of pain echoed in the perfect acoustics of the bathroom. Star was still growling when Bentley had managed to tear away his arm, leaving long vertical gashes where Star's teeth had been.

Blood dripped all over the tile flooring. Bentley was turning a funny shade of green... he gripped his bite with his other hand, biting the inside of his cheek to keep from screaming again. I watched in a slow motion horror as his big black boot swung backwards and Star cowered in front of him, her growl turning into a whimper. Bentley was going to kick her with such a great force that it could kill her if he hit her in the right place... *The wrong place*. The voice in my head corrected.

"No!" I screamed out, lunging forward, my arms reaching out to my Star.

The boot came forward with such force that it knocked me backwards and I heard a sharp cracking noise as it collided with my side.

"Jesus, Mel!" Bentley exclaimed, crouching down beside

me. "What the fuck did you do that for?"

"You were going to kill her," I said between strained breaths. I couldn't breathe right, my side was burning, and adrenaline rushed through my body. I closed my eyes and smiled as I saw Elijah in my head, placing his delicate hands on me, on my side, and healing my wounds.

"*She* was going to kill *me!*" Bentley corrected, reaching for my hands but then pulling away when Star nipped at him.

"You scared her," I explained, unsuccessfully attempting to stand. I winced in pain and curled into a ball.

"And that's supposto justify what she did to me? I don't think so! Mel, tha-"

I started to cry and Bentley stopped talking. Star licked my face, trying to stop the tears. My side pulsated in pain... I wished my blood would stop pumping so hard. With every breath I took it got harder to breath. It felt like there was a cold metal blade stuck in my side, I just wanted it out.

"Fuck, Mel. Just fuck!" Bentley breathed out. "I have steel toed boots," he admitted, cupping his face in his hands.

"I ca-"

"I hurt you, didn't I?" Bentley asked, shaking his head back and forth rapidly.

I nodded, thinking that I could hardly breathe.

"This isn't your fault, Mel. It's not yours, and it's not mine. It's all Star's fault!" he accused.

"Don't you dare blame her!" I shouted, wincing afterward. My face scrunched up in pain, I could feel every cell in my body hurt more with every breath I took. I couldn't even tell where the pain was coming from anymore.

"Damn it, Melissa! This isn't natural! It isn't normal and it sure as Hell isn't right!" Bentley yelled, standing up and pacing back and forth in the bathroom. He rested in fingers on the bridge of his noise as he paused in front of me.

"Mel, we have to put that dog down. We have to kill it. It was her time the day before yesterday. She shouldn't be here... shit, she tried to kill me. Mel, you know it's not what I wan-"

"Is that what you really care about? Star? Bentley, I'm lying on the fucking ground, having trouble breathing! You kicked me, and you don't even ask if I'm okay! Bentley, something is wrong with you," I said, finding the strength to stand up. I leaned over to my left, my hand gingerly resting where Bentley's boot had whacked the shit out of me.

"You know I care about you, baby, that's why I'm here... that's why I'm saying all this! Mel, this is for your safety and mine."

"I can't breathe," I said, doubling over, trying to take slow, deep breaths.

"It's okay, I'll take you to the hospital," Bentley said, taking a step toward me. Star growled and he stopped dead in his tracks.

"Easy girl," he said.

"Easy girl?" I asked, my voice sounded like a whisper. "You just talked about killing her, and you want her to be an easy girl?" I wanted to cough, but I suppressed it because I knew it would hurt too badly.

"Mel, don't talk," Bentley said lifting his hands to his front and placing his palms outwards. His eyebrows inched up and his eyes begged for forgiveness... a forgiveness I wasn't ready to give.

"I'll talk if I wa-"

"No, Mel, I think you punctured your lung, probably by a broken rib or something."

"I punctured a lung? *I* punctured a lung? No, Bentley, *you* punctured my lung and broke a rib or something!" I said slowly. I wished I could yell.

"Please take it easy, Melissa, you're hurt," Bentley said.

"Stop talking about killing my dog! And yes, it's mine. Not ours! We're over, Bentley. Over!" I said, still in a whisper.

"I think you're overreacting a little bit," Bentley said, reaching his hand out to me. I slapped it away, sniffling, trying to stop crying.

"I am not! Now leave me alone!" I cried, picking up Star in my arms, holding her like the little helpless puppy that she was.

"Mel, you have to let me take you--"

"I don't have to let you do shit!" I exclaimed, bustling past him.

I walked up the stairs, ignoring Bentley's pleas and apologizes. I had to go find him... I needed Elijah. He would understand. He would help me. He called to me... His woods called to me.... beckoned me, whispered to me, wanted and desired me.

"Mel, come back here! You're acting crazy!" Bentley called after me. It was no use. I wasn't turning back. I walked steadily into the woods... I couldn't run, but I walked as fast as I could. I darted behind trees, zigzagged through the woods. Bentley didn't stand a chance of catching me.

I found a small clearing in the woods, damp leaves covering the twigs that scattered the ground. Unable to run any farther, unable to breath, my knees gave way and I hugged the ground, my arms stretching up above my head. Star laid down with me, licking my face.

"It's okay, Star," I breathed out, panting heavily. It hurt so badly to breathe that part of me wanted to stop all together. "I won't let anyone hurt you," I promised. Even though it pained me to talk, I felt it was important for Star to know that I loved her, that I would always love her, and that nothing would ever come between us again.

"I know things seem hard right now, but I promise you we'll get through this, girl. Nothing-" I paused, wincing. My eyes closed and I opened them again with a start and took in a sharp breath.

"--nothing will stand in my way," I said, nuzzling my face against hers. I blinked my eyes, though they were closed for much longer than they were open.

"Stay here with me, Star," I whispered. I could barely talk anymore. "I just have to close my eyes for a minute. Then, I'll be better. Then, we'll go back home. Just a-" I closed my eyes, unable to speak anymore. I felt Star sigh as she laid down beside me. The pain in my side was white hot... I could feel the blood pounding around it. I felt a sharp knife stab me every time I took a breath. But none of that mattered, my eyes were closed and I was slowly drifting off into sleep...

I heard footsteps coming from behind me. My face scrunched together, my sleep interrupted. I didn't want to see

Bentley now. How did he even follow me... find me? Why did he even care so much? All he cared about was Star; killing Star... he wanted to kill my poor baby! My eyes jerked open with a flash; I had to be conscious to protect her. My muscles tensed and the pain in my side intensified by ten.

I felt myself relax and my breathing assumed a normal slow speed. It was only Elijah... Bentley was nowhere to be seen. I smiled slightly as I watched Elijah walk towards me, the sun gleaming behind him.

"You look like you just came off the set of a horror movie," he stated, crouching down beside me.

"She came back," I said, feeling strength returning, as he rested his hand on my head, brushing the hair from my face.

"So I see," he replied, the words rolling off his tongue.

"But she was de-"

"Shh, first let's hear about what happened to you," Elijah said, placing a finger up to my lips. I nodded slowly and took in a deep breath, wincing at the pain, but I needed the oxygen.

"It's all Bentley's fault!" I said strongly.

"Bentley?"

"My boyfriend. He freaked out when Star came back... he wanted to kill her! I told him not to hurt her, but he wouldn't listen to me... he didn't care. He didn't care at all! He kicked me, Elijah! He kicked my side and it hurts so badly," I complained, tearing up.

"There, there, my sweet Mel, it's all going to be okay," Elijah promised.

"Why does he always have to wear those stupid-ass work boots? They have a goddamned steel toe... Oh God, it hurts so bad!" I wailed, squirming... the pain was growing worse and all I wanted was to escape it.

"Shh, hold still, please. Will you let me take a look at it?" he asked. I stopped writhing and looked him in the eyes... his glorious, beautiful, entrancing eyes... I nodded.

My heart froze as he slowly lifted up the towel wrapped around me, stopping just below my breasts. I wished I had put on some clothes or at least some underwear before I stormed out of my house. I didn't feel uncomfortable though. Elijah didn't seem to even look at my body... just my wound. Then, he looked into my eyes.

"I can help you, but only if you relax," he said, smiling slightly. I hadn't realized how tense I was until then. I started to take a deep breath, but then stopped myself, remembering how much it would hurt. I closed my eyes and tried to relax all the muscles in my body; ignoring the stinging pain in my side.

I breathed in sharp and strong as Elijah laid his hands on me.

"Mmm!" I muffled a scream. "That hurts," I breathed out.

"I know, Mel, but it's going to be okay." I nodded, closing my eyes tightly and gripping the wet leaves around me. I wished I had something to bite down on... it hurt worse than before... why was he hurting me? Why was I letting him hurt me?

"So, tell me... what's with the bath towel?" Elijah asked with a chuckle. I didn't want to talk, but Elijah was waiting for an answer.

"I was in the shower with Star when Bentley showed up. He scared me, kicked me, and then I ran out here," I explained. The pain in my side was starting to ease. I could feel everything moving, the blood flow slowing, the pain slowly and steadily dwindling down to a slow trickle.

"Just lay here with me while the healing soaks in," Elijah advised. I felt him pull the towel back down over me. I didn't open my eyes... I didn't want to. The world I was in was amazing, pain free, so many colors, so many wonders, so soothing and soft; and it was all because I was with Elijah.

I heard the leaves rustle as Elijah laid down next to me. I wanted to feel his strong arms wrapped around me, but I didn't know how to ask.

"Maybe Bentley was right," I breathed out after a minute.

"Right about what? Mel, I'm not expert on love, but he shouldn't have abused you like that. You deserve better than that."

"No, not that. About Star. Maybe he was right about Star," I admitted, though it was the last thing I wanted to say.

"In what sense?"

"She was dead... and she came back... she was dead. *Dead.* **Dead.** *Dead.*" No matter how many times I said it, it just didn't sound right.

"Was she?" Elijah asked softly into my ear. I felt a warm tingling sensation flow down my entire body, prancing down my spine.

"You saw her."

"Yes. Yes, I did. But she was dead?"

"Yes," I replied with a heavy sigh... I didn't want to talk about this anymore.

"I asked you once before, and I shall ask you again: What's the definition of death, Mel?"

"It doesn't matter... there's no way she could have come back."

"But she did come back, so there must have been a way," Elijah pointed out. Though my eyes remained closed, I could picture his smile perfectly. He was my Elijah... mine.

"It was unnatural. Bentley is right... I have to kill her." It pained me to even think the words, nearly killed me to say them.

"No!" Elijah declared so loudly it made me jump. "No," he repeated a little softer. "Maybe you just have the definition of 'dead' wrong. There's so much out there, so many worlds, so many planes of existence... so much that you can't even fathom."

"Bu-"

"Shh, Mel, rest now. Listen to me. I can open your eyes to a different world, many different worlds. I can redefine your definitions of a lot of things if you allow me to. I want you to let me, Mel. I want to be part of you, your life, your destiny, Mel, I want to be your destiny," Elijah spoke with such clarity, I was sure he knew exactly what he was talking about. Though, it didn't all make sense to me now, I had faith that one day it would.

"Think about it, Melissa. You've known me your whole life." His words echoed in my ears as I drifted off deeper into unconsciousness, allowing the darkness to consume me. I let my guard down and was at peace with the world... trusting everything... trusting Elijah.

Whoo, whoo

"Lee me 'lone," I said, pushing Star away from my face.

Whoo, whoo

"I dun wanna get up," I said, as Star relentlessly pawed at

me. Finally I opened my eyes... where was I? The woods surrounded me.

Whoo, whoo the owl called from the tree. I heard the scurrying of a chipmunk, the clawing of a raccoon, and Star's ever-so-faint whine as she looked in the direction of home.

"Okay, girl, let's go home," I said, standing up with great ease. The pain in my side had vanished as I struggled to remember what had happened.

I shivered in the darkness, wondering how long I had been out here. *My mother must be worried sick about me*, I thought to myself. I wrapped the towel tighter around my body, wishing it were warmer out here.

Star trudged home as if she'd walked this rout a million times over. I was grateful for her... I would have been lost without her. The walk home took around ten minutes, and within that time my buried memories came rushing back to me. Elijah... healing... destiny... had it all been a dream? It had to have been. After all, it wouldn't have been the first time I'd dreamt of him.

The light was on in the living room, the porch light gleamed from one-hundred yards away. I slowly pulled open the screen door; it made a terrible screeching sound. I pushed open the heavy front door and saw my mother staring at me from the couch, papers scattered all over the room.

"Melissa!" she exclaimed, standing quickly and pulling me into a giant bear-hug. "I was so worried about you! How could you possibly run away like that?" she asked, pulling away from the embrace, gripping my shoulders tightly as if that would stop me from running away from her right then and there.

"I'm sorry, mom," I said wearily, I wondered if there was a lecture soon to follow.

"Think of how I felt, Melissa! Coming home to find Bentley bleeding all over my house! Hysterical, talking about you, something about broken ribs and a punctured lung, Star coming back to life, and-" My mother's words stopped short when she noticed Star standing beside me.

"Oh. Dear. God," she said slowly, breathing in deeply, placing her hand on her heart. She said nothing, but returned to the couch. I followed her and sat beside her.

"Mom, listen to me, it's okay. I know it's freaky at first... I'm still pretty wigged out... but I mean, it's okay. She came back... there has to be a reason," I explained, trying to keep her calm. The last thing I wanted to deal with right now was my mom having a heart attack.

"No. No, Mel, it's not okay. This is not natural. It's not good. But it did happen for a reason," my mom said, her words getting faster by the letter.

"A reason, mom," I said, running my fingers through her waist-length hair.

"That boy you met in the woods! How many times have I told you not to talk to strangers? Do you know how hard I have worked to keep you away from bad people?"

"Mom, where is this coming from? He's not a bad person! Bentley is overreacting."

"No, Melissa, you're under-reacting! This is not okay! You cannot see that boy any more. *He* is responsible for this, this, this atroci-"

"Mom!" I yelled. "There's no way he can be resp-"

"Don't tell me what I do and do not know, young lady!" my mother snapped. I'd never heard her talk like this to me before. Sure, we'd had our moments, our fights, our screaming matches, but something about her voice was drastically different. This time, she was serious.

"Mom, I don't understand," I said calmly.

"Mel, it's something I-"

"What's that?" I asked, noticing the details of the papers that were tossed about the room. "Mom! Wh-"

"Honey, I was concerned about you... what Bentley said and how he was acting... this-"

"So you went through my stuff?" I screamed, picking up a picture of Elijah... one from the hidden compartment in my desk drawer.

"Yes. Yes, I did. Mel, I am your parent, a concerned parent, and I needed to know-"

"Needed to know what, mom? Because I'll tell you something you should know!"

"Don't take that tone with me!"

"You've lost my trust. All my trust! I'll draw whoever I want! I'll see whoever I fucking want to see! And I do whatever I please! I'm seven-fucking-tee-"

"Mel, stop it!" my mother warned.

"-nah years old! God, mom! I know it's hard being a single parent... trust me, I get it. But just because dad had the fortitude to leave this hellhole doesn't mean you hav-"

"Melissa! That's enough!"

"-e to take on the role of the overprotective father! Okay?"

"Your father didn't have the fortitude to leave. I fucking left him! I did it for your safety, Mel, and you're going to have to-"

"To what, mom? Trust you? Because as I recall you lost my trust as soon as you violated my personal privacy and ransacked my stuff!"

"I didn't ransack anything! I looked and I found what I was looking for. Mel, you stay away from Elijah! He's not any good! He'll hurt you, Mel. You stay away from him!"

"Like I said, *mother...* " She hated it when I called her "mother." "I'll see whoever I fucking want to see and when I want to see them. There's nothing you can do to stop me!"

"You wanna bet on that? Because you're grounded! You're not leaving the house until you promise to stay away from him! I'll call and cancel your school tomorrow, tell them you're sick. Go ahead and test me!"

"But tomorrow I have cheerleader practice, it's really important! You can't do that!"

"I can and I will. Stay away from him."

"NO!" I screamed, gathering up as many pictures as I could before storming downstairs. I slammed my door shut and locked it.

I slid into my bed, pulling the covers tightly around my body. The tears streamed down my face, they wouldn't stop for the entire night. All I wanted was to be in Elijah's arms. All I wanted was to hear Elijah's voice. All I wanted was--- wait... how did my mother know his name? I hadn't said his name... Oh, whatever! I took a deep breath and screamed into my pillow.

You've know me your whole life. Elijah's words echoed in my eyes. I paused to think... had I? We'd only met yesterday... but I'd had so many dreams of him. And he was at my Granddad's death... how many other memories of him had I buried? I strained to remember, but I couldn't. They were buried for a reason... a reason I had buried as well... a reason my mother refused to tell me... it'd been long buried in her mind, resurfacing only once in a while then she would force it away from her head again. That's what scared her about Star... everything was resurfacing.

Chapter Four
Secrets

The whole world was against me. Even my own mother betrayed me, going through my stuff just because of something my stupid-ass boyfriend said. She didn't trust me. She didn't care about me. She didn't even ask me anything... she just told me this, and told me that... Who did she think she was anyways?

The night was long and cold. The rain slashed against the window, begging me to let it in. The lightning lit up the sky every couple seconds. With each strike, a new memory flashed before me... but as soon as it came, it vanished again. The thunder rolled throughout the sky, creeping past my walls and into my head. It loomed there, no longer frightening as it'd once been when I was younger. I could deal with it now... just like I could deal with so many other things my mother wouldn't trust me with.

I just knew she was hiding something... there was no other explanation! How did she know Elijah's name? I was positive I hadn't said it... why would I? That would give her power... some form to identify him by. Surely, I wouldn't have let something so pertinent slip, even in my fit of anger. No, there was some secret... could she read my thoughts? No, that was crazy... but then again, everything else happening was crazy.

No, wait, I told myself, shaking the unnerving thought of my mother reading my mind. *Think of another logical reason...* I took a deep breath and tried to clear my mind of all other worries, and just focus on the mystery of my mother.

I eventually came to her past... It had to be something about her past! She must have known Elijah... *No,* I thought, bursting my own bubble, *Elijah is my age... how could she possibly know him from her past?...* My mind spun relentlessly. There was no answer to be found... only a mystery.

I hardly knew anything about my mother's past. She never

liked to talk about it. List of things I did know:

1) She got pregnant with me when she was seventeen
2) She never talked to any of her family asides from her father... now that he's passed, I have no interaction with my grandmother, aunts, uncles, cousins, or any other form of family from her past.
3) Apparently, she left my father... contrary to what I've believed for my entire life. And it had something to do with my safety...?

That was about it... and as anyone could plainly see, most of this was discovered by deductive reasoning, not by her talking to me or actually explaining anything along the way.

The rain slowly depreciated into a slight drizzle, droplets racing each other down my window. The lightning slowed with the first sign of daylight. Alas, the night was over. The time for thinking was over... and the time for a short amount of sleep was upon me. I rolled over, closed my eyes, and before I knew it an alarm blared in my ears.

I reached to turn it off, not caring about school, my day, my activities, my mother, or anything other than sleep. Ten minutes later, I heard the door to my bedroom slowly creak open. I kept my eyes closed and pretended not to notice.

"Melissa, I know you're awake," my mother said, shaking my foot just to be sure. "I called you in sick at school. After what happened yesterday, I don't think you should go out. I'm leaving for work now and I will be calling in to check on you periodically throughout the day. I *expect* you to pick up." I wondered how long this was going to go on for? I was annoyed my mother had called me in sick... Heather, the head cheerleader and my best friend, sure wouldn't be thrilled with me. But, I supposed there was nothing I could do about it now.

"The alarm system is all hooked up... if you leave, or if anyone decides to drop by, I *will* know. You are to see no one, especially Elijah." And with that, she left my room and I closed my eyes to catch a few more winks.

I rolled over to glance at my clock. 12:23. I stretched, my

body reaching for a new reality... I didn't escape. I stared at my ceiling for a couple minutes. I didn't want to get out of bed, even though I knew I should. Star was still sleeping soundly beside me. I pulled her closer and whispered that I loved her. I wondered what my mother would say to me about her when she got home from work.

The phone on my bedside table rang, making me jump. I picked it up and held it to my ear for a second.

"Hello?"

"Good, you answered. Are you up?"

"Yeah," I lied. "I've been up for a while... ate a pop-tart for breakfast and now I'm looking for lunch."

"Good," my mother replied... I could almost hear the smile in her voice.

"Well, I'll call again soon, so don't even think about going anywhere!" she barked.

"Okay, mom," I replied, resting the phone against my forehead as she said something else.

"Sure thing," I said absentmindedly.

"Alright, sweetheart, I have to go," she said suddenly, as if her boss had caught her on the phone.

"Okay."

"I love you," my mom said. I hung up the phone.

I knew it was harsh... probably too harsh. And, I knew I would regret it. But, at that moment, it made me feel good. Maybe she would think about her actions and how hurtful they were.

I forced myself out of bed... really it was only because I had to pee. If it'd not been for that, I probably would have stayed in bed for the rest of the day. Not one part of me wanted to face the world. To be honest, I was grateful my mother had called me in sick. I didn't think I could function in a social situation... or any situation that required me to interact with anyone... other than Elijah maybe. I wished I could see him. He would make me feel better... comfort me. *He would never betray you*, the voice inside my head promised. I smiled at that comment because I knew it was true.

The hardwood floor upstairs was cold, and I suddenly

wished I'd put on my slippers before walking up the stairs. I ignored the cold and made my way into the kitchen to start some coffee. Just as I pushed the on button, the phone rang again. I picked it up, rolling my eyes.

"Mom, I'm still here. Seriously, it's not even been five minutes," I said, gritting my teeth. Did she seriously not trust me this much?

"Mel, it's Bentley," the voice on the other line said. I sighed, silently cursing myself for not checking the caller I.D.

"Bentley, we're over and done with... I don't ever want to see you again!" I screamed into the phone, hanging it up. I watched the coffee slowly drip into the pot as the phone rang several times in the background. About the fifth time he called, I answered.

"Would you stop fucking calling me? I'm about to block you and call the police!" I threatened... it was an empty threat. To be honest, I felt flattered he would call so many times just to talk to me.

"Geesh, I just wanted to make sure my best friend was okay... she's like never sick!" It was Heather.

"Sorry, I thought you were Bentley," I admitted sheepishly.

"He's here too, but don't worry, I pushing him away from the phone... after stealing his, of course. He won't be calling you again today." I smiled, super grateful to Heather. I sure owed her one.

"What the hell happened between you two?" she asked. "Because frankly, he's telling the whole school that you're crazy - ouch! Bentley, go away!"

"We'll fix it tomorrow," I said, stirring the cream into my coffee. It wouldn't be the first time Heather and I had to exterminate an ugly rumor. The trick was to act like it didn't bother you, while telling everybody something ten times worse about the person who originally started the rumor. It was no big feat.

"Yeah, no worries, I'm already working it, girl." I smiled. Heather was the best... I didn't know how I could ever think she would be mad at me.

"So, you feeling any better?" The question stumped me for a moment... but then I remember she thought I was sick.

"Not really... I'm having horrible stomach issues. I think it's only a 24-hour bug, though. I'll be there tomorrow, don't worry," I promised.

"Alright... well my lunch is over. I gotta run. I'll call later."

"Talk then," I said, hanging up the phone.

I took a sip of my coffee, even though I knew it would burn me. It was one of those things I did and didn't care about. Coffee was so good... how could one possibly wait for it to be cool enough before drinking it?

Star wagged her tail as she plopped down beside me.

"It's okay, girl. I promise I'll find out what's going on." She smiled at me as if she understood.

I wondered how I would find the answers. Surely, my mother would never talk to me about anything... she didn't trust me with what I knew already, which sure as hell wasn't a lot.

Your mother went through your stuff to find the answers she wanted to know... the voice inside my head spoke to me with such clarity. This was true... *And she found just what she wanted...* the voice went on. I smiled to myself, an idea sparking bright in my mind.

After all, if my mother went through my stuff to find her answers, it seemed only fair for me to reciprocate a similar action to find my answers. An eye for an eye, so to say.

I finished off my still way-too-hot coffee, and headed into my mother's bedroom. I started under her bed, pulling out organized box after box, bag after bag. But, all that was to be found there was a bunch of old pictures from when I was little. I couldn't help but look at most of them... I was so little... so young and happy. My mother was young too, practically still a child herself. I wondered how she could stand getting pregnant so young... I wouldn't be able to handle it. As much as I hated to admit it, I would have had an abortion.

I suddenly felt a different appreciation for my mom... she choose me over her own life. She was my age when she got pregnant... there was so much she hadn't done... so many plans and goals... hopes and dreams. She gave them all up for me... me. And how I was repaying her? By being a bitch and going through her stuff behind her back!

Turnabout is fair play, the voice inside my head said. *Your mother went through your stuff first... she didn't even trust you enough to ask you about it. She took your boyfriend's word over your own.* The grateful feeling was gone.

My eyes started to water as the photograph shook in my hands. I thought back to when the picture was taken. I was eight years old, standing by my mother. We both looked so happy... so young... so different... so... innocent and naïve. I wanted to get lost in the picture. I wanted to go back to that time and stay there. I wanted to escape the reality I was in now.

I rested the picture in my lap. I dabbed my eyes with the bottom of my shirt. Now that my vision wasn't blurry, I could appreciate the picture more. I looked into the background. We were at the park, the swing set was in the background... I noticed a man on the swing set... he was to my left and he was looking right at me. I recognized him at once as Elijah... but, that couldn't be possible. It wasn't possible. He looked exactly the same as he did when I saw him yesterday and the day before. But, this was taken almost ten years ago... This made no sense at all.

I set the photo aside as I put the rest away. The clock read 1:58. I had two and a half hours to find the rest of my answers. I couldn't stop thinking about the photo. How long had Elijah been in my life? Why did he look the same age? Was he a vampire... I remembered reading somewhere that vampires didn't age.

Vampire... no, that was crazy. I wasn't crazy! But what was happening to me was crazy. How would I ever figure this out? There were so many questions... so many answers to be found... so little time.

Where else would my mom hide something she doesn't want me find? I asked myself, thinking hard. I paced back and forth in my mother's room. I'd already gone through her desk... under her bed... in her closet – all the places I'm sure she didn't want me looking.

The attic! The voice inside my head exclaimed. I felt excitement... how could I not have thought of that before? I never went in the attic. It was full of dust, rats, and other creepy and dirty things. Being the neat and clean girl that I was, my mother would never expect me to go up there.

I pulled down the stairs, a dust cloud forming before me. I coughed as I looked up into the very deep, very dark attic before me. I gripped the flashlight tightly in my hands, and started up the stairs. The first step creaked as I placed half my body weight on it. I crossed my fingers, lying them against my thigh, hoping the stairs would hold my weight. I'd have a lot of explaining to do if one was broken and/or I was hurt when my mom got home.

RING! The phone made me jump and then laugh at myself. I rushed over to it, checking the caller I.D. It was my mom.

"Still here, mom," I breathed out in an annoyed way.

"Just checking. I love you, Melissa," she said.

"I love you too, mom," I said, though I didn't exactly say it like I meant it. I hung up the phone. I only had so long to do this.

I climbed into the attic, ignoring the squeaking the stairs made as I climbed them. I shined the flashlight around... to my surprise most of the attic was empty. I could hear the scurrying of rats in the walls as well as on the floor in front of me. I wanted to call Star up here, but I didn't want her to get lost. I felt around for a light switch, or a string to pull. Eventually, I found a string, though pulling it did no good. The light bulb must have blown out. At least I had my flashlight.

I found a box off in the corner. This must be it! This must be what my mom didn't want me to find. I rushed over to it, nearly tripping over something small and furry. But, that didn't matter... I could deal with rats as long as I found what I wanted to and got to take a shower afterward.

I knelt down beside the box, ripping back the moist flaps. The box was old and smelled of mold, as did the contents. I was disappointed to find all inside was old doll clothes of mine back from when I was five.

"Fuck me," I breathed out into the darkness as I let the flashlight slip from my hands. Where could it possibly be? There had to be something more. I knew my mom and she wouldn't just bury everything from her past... sure, she'd done a pretty bang up job pretending like she did... but I just knew there was some sort of connection hidden somewhere.

I hid half of my face in the palm of my hand and breathed out slowly, attempting to think hard. I felt two sticky feet dart across my thigh and I squealed. I shook my legs, scaring off whatever creature it was. I scooted back against the wall, pressing my back up against it, shining the flashlight out toward me. Two beady eyes glared back at me. I stifled another scream and took a deep breath. I told myself it was more scared of me than I was of it. It seemed like the longest staring contest I'd ever had, but eventually it scurried away.

I leaned my head back, breathing out a sigh of relief. My head whacked the wall with a hard thud... and it kept leaning back. I shot my whole body forward, turning and shining the light against the wall. It looked solid as could be... I inched toward it, leery to touch it. I reached out my hand, not sure what to expect. My hand touched the wall... it felt solid... I pushed against... nothing... I pushed harder... still nothing... I pushed with all my might... absolutely no response. No, this made no sense. I sat against the wall again, leaning my head back... my head kept going back as my lower back scooted forward.

I placed my hand above my head and held the board steady as I stood up. Looking at the wall, one of the boards was coming out. With my hands, I continued pushing the board forward until it completely came out.

How clever, I congratulated my mother in my mind. *A pressure contraption... apply the right amount of pressure to more than one spot and tada!* I'd only found it by accident... if one didn't know exactly where it was, they would never find it.

I shined the light into the hole, discovering the wall was hallow. I saw no boxes... no pictures... nothing, it appeared to be completely empty. This made absolutely no sense! I stepped inside the small crevice, and looked right, then left... completely empty. What was this? I heard rats' feet pitter-pattering above my head and I shuttered. I wanted out of there! I wanted a warm shower... I wanted the answers.

I felt dirt fall on my head and I wanted to scream. I looked up above me, shining the flashlight straight up. There were giant beams not but four inches above my head. I saw at least ten rats running across them, stopping and sitting there, staring at me. I took a couple deep breaths and tried to stop my heart from beating straight out of my chest. I hated rats! I hated everything about them... how dirty they were... how their beady eyes never blinked or stopped staring at you... their itty-bitty hands grabbed everything in sight.

I shined my light around, hoping to scare some of the off... That's when it caught my eye... the one specific rat... the one chewing on the corner of something that looked like a very old book that was lying sideways across the beam.

I heard the front door open and shut. My heart froze... it had been locked. I was sure I'd checked it when I got up... I was sure even if I didn't that my mother would have locked it when she left for work. I couldn't breathe; I listened to the footsteps walk in the house and stop. All they would have to do is walk down the hallway to the kitchen and they would see the attic was open... if they came in, I would be trapped.

"Melissa? Where are you?" I heard my mother's voice calling me and I let out a sigh of relief. It was just my mom... my mom! I almost choked on my own spit. I coughed it back. I reached up and grabbed the old book, hiding it inside my baggy pants. I heard the door leading to the downstairs open and my mother's footsteps leave the room. I quickly put the board back into place and clambered out of the attic, closing it up just as my mom re-entered the upstairs.

"Oh! Melissa, there you are," my mother said, placing a hand on her heart. "I thought you might have left."

"You're home early," I said in a monotone.

"Yes, I am. Janie said she would cover for me so I could check on you."

"You don't trust me!" I screamed.

"You kept information from me! Dangerous information! Just how long have you known about Elijah? How long have you drawn his pictures?"

"How do you know his name? It seems like I'm not the only one withholding dangerous information, mom." I said, bustling past her, heading to my room.

"For God's sake, Mel, you *told* me his name." It was my mother's bluffing voice. This only proved my theory... my mom was hiding something from me... and she wasn't about to tell me.

"No. No, mom. I didn't," I said slowly, turning to face her.

"Where were you when I got home? Why didn't you answer when I called your name?"

"I was in the kitchen with my headphones on... I didn't hear you come in," I fibbed... it was a pretty good one too, considering the amount of time I had to come up with it.

"Do you know how dangerous that is?" my mother shouted. "What if it had been someone other than me? They could've-"

"The fucking door was locked, mom! You're the only one with a Goddamned key! You're seriously going to yell at me for listening to music?" I freaked, throwing my arms up in the air.

"Mel, please," my mother sighed, clenching her fists to keep from yelling at me. "I was worried about you. You don't underst-"

"You know why I don't understand, mom?" I asked, biting the inside of my lip with my head slightly tilted. "Because you won't fucking talk to me!"

And, with that, I ran downstairs to my room. I slammed my door and locked it... she wasn't going to sweet talk me out of being mad. She was in the wrong. I was the teenager, she was the mother. She was supposed to tell me what I needed to know, and I was supposed to keep things from her that I didn't want her to know... that was how it worked! It wasn't that hard to see... why couldn't she understand? Why couldn't she trust me?

I threw myself on my bed and blinked back the tears. The deep breaths helped, and soon, I was ready. I was ready to read... whatever this was, I hoped and prayed that it would have the answers. I stared at the book, just lying on my bed, for the longest time. The binding was cracked and the corners chewed by rats. The cover was blank... an off-purple color. I wondered what it could be, but at the same time I didn't want to find out... I'd been disappointed so much lately, I didn't want to be disappointed again. Finally, though, curiosity got the best of me. I picked it up and opened to the first page. My mother's name was written in the top left corner, so neat and clean, much unlike her handwriting now. There was a date and a lot of writing beneath it... could this be a diary?

Tap...tapp...rap-a-tap-tap. The noise made me jump, and I quickly stashed the diary away under my covers. I went over to my door, unlocked it, and opened it.

"I don't wa-" There was no one there. I felt my eyebrows scrunch together as I heard the noise again. I shut the door and it suddenly stopped. I listened... I could hear my mother's faint sobs coming from above me... her room was directly above mine. I felt bad and my heart lurched in my chest... I'd made my mother cry. After all she's done for me, I made her cry.

Tappity-tappity-pat-tap-rap-rapity-rap-tap-tap-tap. It was coming from the window. I slowly approached it, hoping to God it wasn't Bentley. I half-way didn't want to lift up the blinds. But, I finally convinced myself that there was no risk. The window was locked and no one could come in unless I wanted them to.

I lifted up the blinds slowly, ready to let them down again if it was Bentley. But, who I saw standing there was not Bentley... he was not Bentley at all. In fact, the person standing there was the person I most wanted to see. Elijah. He was here for me... to help me... to hold me and love me and care for me.

"Elijah!" I gasped, hurrying to unlock and lift the window.

"Sweet Melissa," he said, offering up a giant smile. He climbed through the window and pulled me in for a warming embrace. I felt the hot tears fill my eyes and I tried to blink them back.

"Shh, it's okay, just let it out," Elijah whispered in my ear. And I did. I cried for a long time, clutching his shoulders as I loved the protective feeling his arms wrapped around me provided. After a while, my sobs subsided and slipped off into the darkness of the night that had overcome us.

I laid on my bed. Elijah sat beside me, looking down at me and smiling. He ran his fingers through my hair and I gazed back up into his intense eyes.

"Elijah?" I asked, loving the way his name sounded when I spoke it.

"Yes?" he replied sweetly.

"Did I really see you yesterday?"

"I don't know, did you?"

"I think so... I mean, you were... maybe it was... did you see me?"

"I see you all the time, Mel. I see you when I close my eyes... when I dream... even just when I think. I find you're on my mind quite often." I smiled, my heart beginning to warm. The bitterness my mother had instilled inside me was slowly vanishing with every word Elijah spoke.

"But in reality...?"

"If you saw me, you saw me. Dreams are a certain type of reality too, Mel," he answered, soothingly running his fingers down my neck, trickling down my arm, and grabbing my hand. He squeezed it as he winked at me.

"I feel like I've known you my whole life," I said slowly, carefully choosing my words.

"You have. We've known each other for that long. For, I must not be the only one dreaming of the other."

"You dreamt of me too?" I asked, sitting up. Elijah nodded and I felt a smile creep across my face and my eyes brightened. Suddenly, I felt a foreboding feeling sneak inside me. My eyes stung from crying too much and I just wanted to close them. I needed sleep...

"What's wrong?" Elijah asked.

"If I show you something-"

"Of course," he promised before I could finish. I reached into my pocket and pulled out the photo I'd found earlier under my mom's bed.

"Is this you? And if so, how is that possible? I mean it was tak-"

"Melissa," Elijah breathed out with a slight chuckle. "Settle down. There's a lot to be learned... there's a lot just waiting to be uncovered. There are a lot of secrets that you are now ready to know. *I* will tell them to you, my sweet Melissa, because I *trust* you."

"My mother doesn't trust me... she doesn't like you," I said sympathetically... how could she not like Elijah? He was amazing.

"Your mother lives in a great deal of fear... she doesn't know the whole of everything, she can't see the bigger picture."

"I don't follow you," I admitted.

"There's a lot to follow... and you need sleep."

"Not as much as I need the truth," I demanded.

"When fear rules a person, they become completely different. They do things they would never do before... they think things that are completely wrong... they jump to conclusions."

"Bu-"

"Was your mother afraid when Star came back?"

"Yes." My eyes stung like hell. I blinked them a couple times, loving the cooling sensation closing them allowed.

"Did she yell at you as if you'd done something wrong? Did she bring something completely irrelevant into the conversation because she was thinking weird things? Did she jump to conclusions?"

"Yes."

"A prime example. I know you want all the answers now, Mel, but you need sleep... otherwise, it will just frustrate you." I nodded. He was right. He was always right.

I pulled the covers around me and closed my eyes. I felt the bed move as Elijah stood up and I heard his footsteps heading toward the window.

"Elijah, wait!" I said, forcing my eyes open.

"Yes?"

"Will you stay with me?" I breathed out.

"As you wish," Elijah replied, the words rolling off his tongue. My mind went straight to *The Princess Bride* and a smile formed on my face for the final time that night.

My heart fluttered as Elijah crawled under the covers with me. I felt his arms wrap around me, lingering above my breasts, but then moving down to my waste without making contact above. I breathed out slowly... I wanted him to feel me. I wanted to kiss him... to kiss lots of different parts of him. But I couldn't... I was too tired. My eyes stung, my brain ached from too much thinking, my muscles were all sore, and I needed sleep.

I pressed my back against his abs... spooning felt so good.

I closed my eyes again, and allowed myself to completely let down my guard, become completely vulnerable, and fall into a deep, dark world of dreams.

Chapter Five
The Past

No big surprise, when I awoke Elijah was nowhere to be found. The early morning wind drifted in through my window. I shuddered in the cool air as I walked across my room to close the window. The morning sun hadn't begun to cast its colors over the North Carolina mountain range, though it threatened to start at any minute.

I wondered if I was going to go to school today. I wanted to... but at the same time, I didn't feel like I could face the world. My entire life was being shaken at its roots... it's secret roots that I know nothing about.

As I climbed back into bed, pulling the comforter around me, my thoughts drifted to my mother's journal... and then to Elijah. Who was he? Why was he here? Where did he come from, and why wasn't he in school? Well, the last one was easy enough to answer. So many people around here homeschooled that it wouldn't surprise me if Elijah was one of them. Why did he have to disappear like that? Had he even been here in the first place? I wished he didn't have so many secrets... then again, I could wish the same thing about my mother.

Knowing my mind would never allow me more rest, I picked up my mother's journal and turned to the first entry. I had a couple hours before I had to be up for school... before my mother would come to wake me. I had time, and I needed to know.

The first entry was from around eighteen years ago...

I'm not used to keeping a journal. I never thought I would... I'm not quite sure where to start. The beginning was much too long ago... but, the reason I started keeping this journal is because of what I found out yesterday. It's really big, and I'm not sure how I feel about it. Part of me is happy... part of me wishes that it's not true, but I know it is. I can feel it.

Yesterday, I returned to the doctor's office to end my secretive visits. He told me... he was happy for me... he smiled more than me. It's not that I'm not happy, or won't love it, it's just... it's so big. I wasn't expecting to be expecting.

Alex doesn't know yet... I'm not sure how to tell him. I'm a month in, and he didn't even know it was a possibility. I'm planning on telling him this weekend at the senior trip to Misty's lake house. Misty's been through all of it with me... since the day I lost my virginity. I don't know what I would do without her shoulder to cry on.

They'll be three couples going, me and Alex, Misty and Abe, Jace and Kris. We've been the steady couples since sophomore year... here we are now, our last hurrah before we make our separate ways in life, starting out on our own. I guess my plans are blown now... after all, I am keeping it. There's no way I could live with myself otherwise.

So that was what it was like for my mother when she found out she was pregnant with me... I guess it wasn't as bad as I'd pictured it. I figured she would probably have cried a lot, debated an abortion or adoption. At least I knew she wanted me... even if she was overwhelmed... but then again, who wouldn't be? Seventeen is a young age to start a family. Too young.

The next day:
The fresh air up here is rejuvenating... well worth the tedious seven hour drive. The lake water is cool and eases the sunburn on my shoulders. I can't stop thinking about telling Alex... it doesn't feel right. He keeps talking about our future plans, how happy he is to be with me, how wild and crazy we'll be in college. I don't think I'm going to college any more. I don't know how I could...

This is going to wreck Alex... I don't know how he'll cope... then again, I still don't know how I'll cope. Part of me wants to keep this from him, but I know that's wrong. I have to tell him... I'll tell him tonight, when we're alone in our room. He's gone right now with Krissy. They're driving to his uncle's who supposedly has a keg he'll sell us.

The day after that:
I didn't tell him last night... he ended up getting drunk and it didn't feel like it was the right time to tell him. I didn't drink... I couldn't do anything that could possibly harm my child. Everybody but Misty gave me shit about it, but it was worth it. I love my child already... I'm so attached to it. I mean, it's actually growing inside my body.

Alex is hung-over... we're hoping a quick dip in the lake will be enough to get over it. I'll tell him tonight, for sure.

Later that day:
Well, I told him... but, it wasn't how I expected it to go. In fact, all of the events

that took place today were unexpected, and I suspect some of them to be a figment of my imagination.

I'm not sure where to start, so I'm going to write slowly and jot down every single thing I remember happening.

We were down by the lake, laughing and having a great time. I was the only sober one... I considered doing some weed because I've known girls who were pregnant and did that, but I decided against it. I want to be completely drug-free for my baby.

I'm a pretty good swimmer, so I decided to dive from this rock that was really high up. Half way down, I had the weirdest thought... the most peculiar feeling that I shouldn't have done that. "My future has changed." The thought hurtled through my head as I hit the water with a hard, yet elegant, splash.

The world under the water was different... everything was dark and murky when it shouldn't have been... I mean, I hadn't stirred the water that much. Nevertheless, I loved it down there. The water felt so good... the strange silence of the water filled my ears as I felt a wave vibrate throughout my body. I never wanted to resurface... though, that feeling would soon change.

After I couldn't hold my breath any longer, I slowly made my way to the surface of the water. I was jerked back just below it... I could feel something... someone?... tugging at my ankle. I pulled my foot back, shaking it around, trying to kick it... him?... in the face. My hands flailed above me, my fingertips grasping at the cool air above the water. I let out what was left of my breath and desperately tried to make my neck longer. I barely made it above the water, sucking in a deep breath that consisted of half-air half-water.

I looked down at my ankle, but the water was too murky to make out what was holding me back.

"Help!" I called out, though I'm sure my friends only heard a quick shout as the current splashed against me, filling my mouth with water. My lungs couldn't take it... I was starting to choke... I was being suffocated. I thrashed about in the water, unable to get free. I could only hope one of my friends would notice me. I'd been quiet — much too quiet — about diving off of that rock.

"Please help me!" I thought, trying to send out a telepathic message to Alex.

"I can help you," a calm and soothing voice came from inside my head. I shook my head... I was hearing things... my vision was slowly fading as I gulped down more water in a pitiful attempt to get air.

"Please!" I begged to whatever source there was out there trying to help me. I was drowning, but that didn't matter... my baby was drowning! If I didn't make it... my baby wouldn't make it.

"I can help you and your daughter,"

the voice came once more. I tugged desperately at my ankle, trying to free it from the death-grip.

"Okay, please help me!" I thought, I couldn't let my baby die.

"There will be a price... there's always a price, but that's not a bad thing," the voice said... it was much too calm for the situation I was in. How could he be so nonchalant about all this? It was as if he controlled death.

"Sure, whatever price, just get my baby out alive."

"Ahh, your daughter. You don't know this yet, but she's a beauty," the voice said in almost a reminiscent tone.

"Help me! Help me! Oh, please, God, help me!" The words screamed in my head as I gasped for more air, my hands reaching for life just above that shallow line of water. I could see the sun beating down... my fingertips could feel the air I needed. My head pounded and my lungs were filled with water... Although, I hadn't ever been that close to death before, I knew I was close to dying.

"You must promise me whatever I want, in order for me to help you... though, you'd better hurry, you don't have much longer now," the voice said, confirming my suspicions.

"I promise!" I screamed in my head... anything... anything to get me out alive. "I promise you anything you want!" They were dangerous words, but death was also dangerous.

"Good," the voice said, and then I saw his face. It was so clear, so vivid... I had to sketch it as soon as I was conscious again. He smiled at me... at us, my daughter and I... he knew it was girl... or is it a girl? I don't even know, but he sounded so sure.

I felt my body go limp and all else around me faded as I drifted back into the depths of the water.

The next thing I remember is Alex's voice, pleading for me to come back. My eyes darted open.

"I'm pregnant!" I shouted as I sat up, coughing out water.

"Oh, thank God you're alive!" I heard. I was overwhelmed with the amount of hugging, crying, and thanking God that was going on around me. I wondered if Alex had heard me...

"And you stopped breathing... and then Alex did CPR, but then we couldn't get your heart beating either, and then... well, you're back! Oh, you had us so worried!" Misty was saying, crying all over me. I pulled her close and told her that I was okay.

"I'm pregnant," I repeated, staring at Alex.

"I heard you," he said, smiling at me, looking deep into my eyes.

"You're not shocked?" I asked.

"I could tell... and Misty's freak out as you were drowning confirmed my suspicions."

"Yeah, sorry, I kind of screamed that

you were pregnant a lot..." After that, there was a lot of congratulating and rejoicing. But, through all that, I couldn't get the picture of that man out of my head.

I haven't told anyone else about him... I have my doubts that he's even real. I mean, I was drowning... my brain lacked the oxygen that it needed, so it's a more than rational explanation that I hallucinated it all. But, on top of all that, it just doesn't feel right to tell anyone about him. He's mine... and nobody else has to know. Nobody else should know. It feels wrong in a right way, if that makes any sense at all.

My hands shook and my head throbbed... that was exactly how I felt about Elijah. I knew exactly what my mother meant. But, it wasn't possible for that to be Elijah... Elijah was so young... so into *me*. My mother must have imagined this... maybe she'd just seen too many horror movies. Yeah, that was it. The nagging doubt wore at my mind, destroying bits and pieces of it... my theories had all gone to Hell. I had no choice but to keep reading.

I skimmed a few pages and entries, but there was nothing interesting in them... just normal pregnancy stuff. That is, until I reached month four.

I dreamt about him tonight. He came to me through a dream. I'd almost forgotten about him... I want to forget about him. He gives me a feeling that words can't describe. He wants something... someone. I don't remember everything about the dream. I just remember sitting there, my hand over my baby-belly, thinking about how much I love this child already. He approached me with a swagger and rested his hand on my shoulder.

"How's our little girl doing?" he asked, bending down to kiss my tummy.

It was then I awoke, covered in a cold sweat. Alex by my side, sleeping soundly.

I can't tell anyone about this... they'll call me crazy... who knows what would happen. I have to be here for my baby. I have to put this as far from my mind as possible.

The dreams continued in a monthly pattern, each having the same type of experience. I didn't understand... who could this be? Why did he keep calling me his? Was he my father? My true father?... maybe that was why my mother left Alex. But, I hadn't even gotten to that yet. My mom just kept talking about what a bright future her and Alex would have... he even proposed. He did everything right... he sounded so sweet. But this... this guy... no, monster, was tearing everything apart; driving my mother crazy slowly. Who was he? Was he even real? Maybe my mom was schizophrenic... that would explain her extreme paranoia... and her freak out when she found out about Elijah. Maybe it just triggered something familiar?

I had her today. A beautiful baby girl, healthy, happy, wonderful. She didn't even cry when she came out. The nurses held her for me to see, though then they quickly wheeled her away and gave me something more for the pain.

I awoke several hours later and demanded to go and see her in the nursery. I was the only parent in there. I watched her sleep... she looked so peaceful and happy. She was my Melissa.

As I reached to pick her up, my hands were met by another pair... they were strong, big, and held my hands so carefully, as if they were the most fragile thing in the world. I looked up to Him.

"I told you she was beautiful. She's the most beautiful girl in the world... just wait until she gets older," he said, smiling down at her.

"Is this another dream?" I asked curiously, trying to make eye contact with him.

"No. This is reality," he scoffed, as if I'd asked the craziest question in the world.

"What's your name? Why are you here? I don't even–"

"But you do. You remember me from the water... you sketched me, you dream about me all the time. We made a deal, remember?"

"What's your name?" I demanded to know.

"Elijah," he stated, the name rolling off his tongue.

I stared at the name... unable to read any further. This couldn't possibly be the same Elijah... it had to be a coincidence... right? There was no way... no possible way!

You said that about Star coming back too... Elijah's voice echoed in my ears.

It was just a coincidence, I told myself over and over again... this was just the trigger that set my mother off.

Elijah fit him perfectly, yet I wasn't exactly sure why or how.

"I want to be the first to hold her," he stated, picking her up before I could protest. The way he looked at her was amazing... she was so delicate, so important. She opened her eyes to look at him... He thought she opened her eyes for the very first time. He thought that he was the first thing that she saw. My heart felt sad, I wanted to hold her first. I deserved to hold her first... I was her mother!

What I don't tell him was that my father had already held her – that she had already seen him. It's a secret I will take to my grave.

After a few moments, Elijah handed her to me, and everything else in the world faded away. She was the most magnificent miracle... there was no other way to describe her. My magnificent miracle, Melissa.

"I got here as fast as I could," I heard a voice, panting, by the doorway. I turned to see Alex.

"Alex!" I exclaimed, rushing over to him. I went to introduce him and Elijah, but that was when I noticed that Elijah had disappeared. I stood there, baffled, for just a moment.

"I'll be back, don't you worry. After all, I have to claim what's mine... you gave me the most magnificent miracle I could have hoped for. Thank you,"

"No!" I screamed aloud, clutching Melissa tightly, holding her to my heart.

"What?" Alex asked.

"Oh, I'm sorry, I just got to pick her up. But, here, your her father," I said, passing her to Alex. He smiled at her, but not nearly in the way Elijah had... She was what Elijah wanted... why did he want her? He couldn't take her from me!

She is mine... my magnificent miracle, not his. He would never have her. Ever.

"We're going to be so happy together," Alex whispered to me, leaning in for a kiss.

*   *   *

Later that night, as I watched Melissa sleep soundly, I realized there was only one thing I could do. I had to get away. I had to protect my baby girl... it was the only hope. I had to drop everything... all my contacts... my entire family... even Alex. I could only trust myself. I had to keep her safe.

So, I wrote a letter to my father. There was no way I could just abandon him. I told him I would call once in a while to keep in touch, but that he couldn't tell anyone else.

I sent it in the mail so he wouldn't receive it until I was long gone.

I kissed Alex on the forehead after I finished packing my suitcase and emptied his wallet.

And then, I left.

So, here I am now... at the train station. I'm going out East, as far away as I can get from California. It's for the best. I have to go. I can't let Elijah have her... she's mine.

I turned to the next page, but only to find it blank, along with the rest. I took all this in, not knowing what to think. So many questions were answered... so many unanswered... some possibly without any answer.

I thought about what to do... I wondered if my mom would ever be honest with me... I wondered what Elijah would say about all this.

There was a sharp gasp and I looked up to see my mother standing in front of my bed. I had been so enthralled in my thoughts, that I didn't hear her come in my room to wake me.

"Is that my journal?" she asked slowly.

"Yes, and I've already read it," I admitted, not ashamed.

"We need to have a really long talk," my mother said, unexpectedly calm, and sat down beside me.

"What's your first question?" she asked.

"Why did you keep all this from me?"

"It was for your own good, Melissa. I couldn't explain it all without you thinking I was crazy. I know this is big, and probably really hard for you to understand... but I have your best interests at heart." I nodded, trying so hard to understand everything... my mind swirled with questions, but one stood out more than the others.

"Is my Elijah and your Elijah the same Elijah?" I asked. My mother took in a deep breath and silence filled the air before her answer...

Chapter Six
Two Sides

"I can't believe this is happening," I said, running my fingers through my long hair. My breathing was irregular and I swore my heart was having palpitations.

"I know this is a lot for you to take in, Mel, but you have to try and understand," my mother said comfortingly, placing her delicate fingers on my shoulders. I turned to face her, and, unable to hold it in anymore, I let out a soft cry. The tears streamed down my face, cutting my cheeks with my mother's harsh past.

"What is he?" I asked. My mother only let out a not-so-comforting sigh.

"Mel, listen, I know there must be a million questions running through your head, but I can't tell you anything. You'll be safer if you don't know and just forget about him."

"So, what? You're not even going to talk to me about this?" I asked. I could feel the anger seething through my thin milky skin.

"Please try and under-"

"No, mom! Don't you see? Not communicating about this is what got us into this mess in the first place."

"No," my mother adamantly disagreed. "Elijah is what got us into this mess. If you refuse to talk to him, it will all be fixed."

I sat there for a very long time. I tried to think, but my mind was filled with white noise. The tears dried and the white noise soon turned to worry upon realization.

"You promised me to Elijah?" I asked, my eyebrows scrunching together.

"No, I promised him something an-"

"No, you promised him me. He said 'our girl,' he's come to collect. What does he want with me?" I asked.

"Mel, just don't talk to him anymore! Do you understand me?" my mother screamed. I nodded, tears filling my eyes again.

"Good, now you need sleep. I'm off to work. Stay home from school again, and give me your phone. You need a day by yourself," my mother said, holding out her hand. I placed my phone in it, thinking I didn't know my mother at all... never in a million years would I have dreamt she would act this way.

"Have a good day," I absentmindedly said as she walked out of my room. I muttered an "I love you" but I'm not even sure if either of us registered that it came out of my mouth.

The minutes ticked by, slowly and steadily turning into a couple hours. I wondered what would become of me? If I was promised to Elijah – this obviously higher being – then surely he wouldn't give up just because I refused to talk to him. Besides, how could I possibly do that? Elijah was part of me, he had been there my entire life. He didn't seem bad. Mysterious? Yes. Bad? No.

Even after reading my mother's journal a second time, I still had so many questions. Questions I once thought she would answer, but now, apparently, she wouldn't. Was there any way to find the answers?

I know the answers. Elijah's voice chimed in my ears. I jumped, then took a deep breath. I found his words soothing in a weird way. *I have a whole side of the story you don't know of... your mother has many secrets that even her journal won't divulge. You must know her soul to know her secrets – lucky for you, I know her soul inside and out.*

I wished I knew exactly what he was talking about... I wished I knew exactly what he *was.*

Come to me, Melissa, he called. *Come to me in my woods... I will tell all and your mother never has to know.* He promised me. I could almost feel his strong hand delicately placed on my shoulder to sooth me. As I opened my eyes to jump off the bed and grab my coat, I saw him standing in front of me.

"I was goin-"

"I know," he said with a smile, taking a seat on my bed. He patted next to him, and I obeyed, sitting next to him.

"What do you..." I paused for a very long time. Elijah patiently waited, acting as though time was standing still. "Want with me?" I finally finished.

"Oh, Melissa, you must be absolutely terrified," he stated smoothly, placing a hand on my thigh, as if that was supposed to make everything all better.

He continued, "Want with you? Melissa, I don't want anything *with* you. Search your heart, you know I'm not a creep."

"Do I?" I asked, beginning to doubt my innermost feelings. What did I know about Elijah? He was an enigma.

"You do. You just need a little reassuring. Perhaps my side of the story will help."

"Yes, please tell me your side," I breathed out. Relief washed over me as I realized someone was willing to talk to me about what clearly revolved around me.

"Well," Elijah hesitated. The gut ball returned to my stomach... was I ever going to find out about my own life? I had a right to know! I deserved to know. I wasn't an innocent little kid anymore; I was fully capable of understanding.

"I can't tell you," he breathed out in a huff. I bit the inside of my cheek and wondered if yelling would do any good.

He said, "but, I can show you."

"Show me?"

"If you'll let me, that is," he looked deep into my eyes – as if searching my inner-self for an answer. I nodded subconsciously. He placed his hand against my cheek, moving his thumb slightly. He whispered, "close your eyes and trust me." I obeyed.

Instantly, I was transformed – I could see a different world... an older world tinged with sepia as the colors adjusted to normal around me. I felt my heartbeat regulate and my breathing slowly begin. I watched as a very young image of my mother walked up to a house with a boy... my father?... open the screen door to the porch, and sit down on the swinging bench.

"Are you sure you're ready for this?" He asked. My mother nodded and they began kissing. It went on for a while until they retired inside the house, not taking a genius to figure out where it all led.

Images of myself flashed in my mind – images of being created, being inside my mother's belly, growing up, I even caught tiny glimpses of the future. When the sideshow stopped, I was sitting by a lake... though the reflection wasn't me – it was Elijah.

There was a sudden jerk, and then I was on my own... watching from a 3rd eye that didn't even really exist. Another jerk and I was back in my bedroom, Elijah sitting next to me.

"Please, you must trust me," he said, looking back into my eyes. I looked away.

"Was I just you?"

"Yes, you were... you saw what I saw the night you were conceived. As you know, I felt you come into existence. I felt you reach out – I knew you were there before anyone else ever did. Melissa, I can feel people's emotions... I can read minds... I *know*. But you, I can't get a beat on you. Your thoughts are you own, I can only pick up on a few here and there... piecing them together is impossible. I don't know why, but you're special, Melissa. I knew I had to get to know you, that's why I saved you when your mother tried to kill you."

"What are you talking about?"

"Melissa, your mother was scared... she didn't want you. It doesn't take a genius to know you shouldn't dive off a high cliff when you're pregnant... do you know how easy it would have been for her to have a miscarriage? If it hadn't been for me, she would have. She made that deal because she got scared for her own life."

"That's not what her journal said," I claimed, my heartbeat daring to pound out of my chest.

"You really think she would write something like that in her journal?" Elijah asked, throwing his arms out to his sides. "A journal that you could – and did – find?"

I shook my head slowly, reality hitting me hard.

"How can you do that?" I asked. "I mean, what are you?" I was scared to find out the answer... part of me didn't even want to ask, but I knew it was something that I had to find out.

Elijah sighed and then said, "Melissa, I need to know if you're really ready to find out... are you sure you want to know the answer?"

I bit my lip, my mind delving deep into my thoughts... my

mind swirling with "yes" then "no" and then uncertainty...

"Yes," I finally breathed out. "I'm ready."

"I am Death... like the Grim Reaper only not so cliché and I have more powers. There is a clock on everything with an expiration date – but I have the power to bring things back, like your dog. Death isn't the end, Melissa, it's merely the beginning."

"Death?" I asked. My lungs felt compressed and I didn't know what to say. No matter what he said – I knew he wanted something from me... what did Death want from me?

"Why me?" I asked.

"Because you're special. I couldn't let you go... even if it's a new beginning, you deserved a good life. I wanted to watch you grow up, become the very important person you were born to be. You have a place here, Mel, and I intend to see you get there. You are very dear to me."

"Dear to you? Like a daughter? Or something else?" I asked, not sure which answer I truly wanted to hear.

"Melissa, I didn't know how I would grow to love you that First Night. It's changed so many times as I don't wish to complicate your life... but, I just can't help it, Melissa, I love you lik-"

"I love you too!" I breathed out, meeting him in a warm embrace. I didn't know why or how I trusted him so much – why I felt the way I did... all I knew was that it felt right. ***Do only that which is right.*** The words echoed in my head as my hands slid up and down Elijah's back and his mimicked mine.

"There is a balance," he said suddenly, jerking me away from the blissful world I'd been sucked into.

"A balance?" I asked. Elijah nodded.

He said, "I saved your dog's life. I don't want you to think that you owe me because saving your life was the best thing I ever did... but there's a balance that must come from it...."

"What are you saying?"

"Melissa, I know this is hard for you. But, especially if we are going to be romantically involved, I'm going to need there to be a balance."

"What balance? And what does Star have to do with this?"

"Star is different... and soon it will start to show. Both of you were supposed to die, and I got in the way of that. Like I said, I don't regret it, but I also don't have to deal with the repercussions."

Repercussions? I thought to myself. *How bad are these repercussions?*

"What are you saying?" I asked, wondering what I had to do to bring balance about – but not entirely wanting to know the answer.

"You have to sacrifice a life – someone who's connected to Star."

"Bentley," I sucked air in, coughing on it. "No," I said definitively. "Get out!" I demanded. This was all way too much for me. I couldn't take it anymore. I stood up so my back was to Elijah. What was happening with my life? Why was all this going on? I missed my old life... my normal life... but, then again, had my life ever been normal? I'd always been haunted by Elijah. I didn't know a life without him... maybe it was time to start that life.

I turned back around to face Elijah, but he had already vanished. I rushed over to the landline phone in my bedroom and I dialed Bentley's number.

"Bentley!" I said, sounding way too desperate, upon his answer.

"Mel?"

"Yes, it's me. I'm so sorry for everything that happened. Can we just start over? Please? Will you meet me at the graveyard soon? I'm ready to finally... you know, make love." I said, bees buzzing in my tummy. I needed to do this – this teenagery yet grown up thing. Something normal... something that would take my mind off of Elijah for a long time. Something to get my life back on track. Being with Bentley was the only way I knew how to do that.

Chapter Seven
Today

Present Day:

Second thoughts about going all the way with Bentley tumble through my head as I make my way through the foreboding night. I can hardly believe who I am these days. So much as changed in so little time. I feel as though my history has been torn apart and replaced with a completed foreign one. I don't actually want to lose my virginity to Bentley... I begin to wonder why I called him in the first place. My head starts to pound and my stomach feels uneasy as I think about what's in my left hand. I can't do this.

I reach our spot in the old graveyard. Bentley is late. I lay out the blanket I brought and slip the content of my left hand under it discreetly. Then, I wait. The darkness of the night beats in my heart, filling my veins with fear. I can hear everything around me... the frogs by the lake, the chirping crickets, the rattling of the leaves as the wind shakes the trees. A whoosh of invigoration overcomes me as I realize the night is alive.

I can suddenly feel him watching me. I literally sense his presence. He followed me here to watch, and I now know I can do this. He needs to see it. He needs to know where I stand. He needs to know what side I'm on. Confidence fills me as Elijah's eyes burn into me from the bushes.

"Mel, I'm sorry," Bentley's voice echoes behind me.

"Don't be, it's all my fault," I say with an insincere smile.

"What did you do about it?" he asks. There's no need to ask what he's talking about.

"I brought *her* to the vet to have put down," I lie, carefully putting an emphasis on "her." No matter what happened, Star isn't an "it."

"I'm proud of you," he says, cupping my face with his

rough hands and kissing me. I do my best to kiss him back and ignore the loud scoffing noise from the woods.

"What the fuck was that?" He asks, breaking our kiss.

"I told you I don't like it when you cuss," I say, sitting up and looking around the night. I hear it too. I hear it scurry over to my side. I look at Bentley, but he doesn't see me. His head is turned the other way. Even without looking at his face, I know his eyes are frantically searching for something... anything that seems out of the ordinary. I know he is scared. He doesn't handle fear as well as I do. I assume I handle it better because I read more horror than he does. But then again, it makes me awful jumpy sometimes when I really do get freaked out. The full moon lights the graveyard enough to make out the, far and few between, tombstones. It's a fresh graveyard, which gives it a more and less eerie feeling at the same time.

"It was probably just a squirrel, love," I say, pressing my chest up against his back and wrapping my arms around his neck. He looks back at me and kisses my cheek.

"Are you sure there's nothing out there?" He asks.

"No," I say honestly. I can't resist the temptation to make him a little more scared. It is always entertaining to me to watch people freak out over nothing.

"Babe!" He says, his grip on my hand getting tighter as we hear a growling noise.

"It's probably just a squirrel," I repeat myself, this time trying to convince myself as well.

"Squirrels don't growl like that," he states with a heavy sigh. As much as I hate to admit it, he's right... and it's starting to freak me out too.

"Maybe we shouldn't be out here... it has to be like midnight by now," Bentley says, looking at me with pleading eyes.

"You *know* we're not supposto be out here," I tease, thinking of earlier that night when we sneaked out of our houses to meet there.

"Yeah, but I mean, maybe we're *really* not supposto be out here. Something feels wrong."

"Since when do you have a sixth sense?"

"You know what I mean, Melissa , I know you feel it too. I know you're wigged, weather you admit it or not." Sometimes I hate that he knows me so well. I nod, but the thought of walking home alone makes my stomach knot up. I bite my lip and my eyes shift around my surroundings.

"What's wrong?" Bentley asked.

"I'm just turned on, that's all," I lie, crossing my fingers so it doesn't really count. Besides, I am turned on. We were making out for a while.

"You're scared to walk home, aren't you?" he asks.

"Maybe," I admit.

"Mel,"

"Okay, I am. What's that mean?"

"Absolutely nothing, I'm scared too." I jump as my peripheral vision catches something but, when I jerk my head, I see nothing.

"Well what do we do, we can't exactly both walk each other home. And if we're caught by our parents we'll be dead."

"Maybe not the same kind of dead we'll be if we stay," Bentley says. The mention of the thought that is on both our minds causes a solid line of fear to shoot through my head. The fear is making my adrenaline rush and it feels good soaring through my veins. I lay my head back and smile, taking in a cool breath of the night air.

"It's not funny, Mel," Bentley warns. I don't think Bentley gets the same rush off fear that I do. I wonder for a second if I am normal. Maybe my mind is corrupt from all the horror books that I read. I wouldn't put it past myself. Sometimes, I have some awfully weird and horrid thoughts inside my head. They never last for long, and I don't mean the half of them, but I have them nevertheless.

"Don't you love the way it feels?" I ask, my hands running up and down the damp grass beneath me.

"The way what feels?" Bentley asks, laying down next to me.

"Adrenaline... fear... being afraid. It makes your head go funny and your stomach twist into a knot making you just wanna squirm, and your heart starts beating fast and you can't stop it.

You're scared, but not scared enough to actually start screaming. It's purely indescribable."

"Sometimes you scare me, you know that?" He chuckles to himself in a nervous way. I roll on my side and look at him longingly, knowing what I have to do. It feels so right, so natural, it will give me the best rush of all. It will feel ten times as amazing as how I feel now. I take in a deep breath and hold it. Bentley scoots toward me again, wrapping his arms around me.

My hands feel their way up and down his muscular arms. He pulls me closer and my hands wander behind him. I press myself against him, reaching as far as I can with my arms. I feel around the damp grass and slide my hand under the blanket we lay on. That is where I keep it... just in case... just in case I'm up to it. Just in case I actually decide to do it. Earlier that night, I thought I wouldn't be able to... I didn't think I would be wrong... I didn't think I'd actually go through with it... My stomach gets all knotted up as I think about doing it. But the mere thought of how it will make me feel is enough to set my mind at ease. I know he'll never see it coming. I know he'll be surprised. I know I have to do it. It's the only thing to do.

Chapter Eight
Choosing a Side

I reach for the hand-sickle I placed under the blanket, telling myself that I can do this. My heart pounds as Bentley tears my head toward his.

"I love you, Mel," he says. It throws me. I don't know why I wasn't expecting it. I know he doesn't mean it. How could he love me after everything he did to me? I know I don't love him back because of what I'm planning on doing... because of who I really do love... because of who I am doing this for.

I can't take it anymore and I pull out the hand-sickle. I raise it high above my head. I see my reflection sparkle in Bentley's wide eyes. I feed off of his fear – it's filling me with confidence. Every part of me is screaming at me to finish it – to prove myself to Elijah. But, instead, I relish in the moment, enjoying every last second.

"Mel, what the fuck?" he screams, trying to back away. But I'm too strong for him. He's helpless... and in my clutches. I should just put him out of his misery, but I'm loving the fear, enjoying the struggle. I feel a devilish smile cross my face crawl across my face... it isn't mine. This isn't me. I'm not the same, and once I do this, I never will be. I know that, and I'm okay with it because this is right. This is the time.

The hand-sickle comes down with a slash – slicing Bentley's face open like a ham on Easter Day. The blood splatters on me and I love it. I can smell it and it fills me with the most empowering feeling one can experience. I am in charge of life and death. I am in complete control of something that is not me. I decide whether it lives or whether it dies. And now, I want it somewhere in-between.

Its screams fill the air, but only Elijah and I can hear it, and neither will help. Blood gushes from it and I wonder how long it would take if I just let it bleed out. A shrill laugh fills the air and rings in my ears. I'm surprised to find that it comes from inside me. It's my heart screaming at me... asking me what I'm doing, and begging me to stop; for my old self to snap back. But I won't. I refuse to. This feels too good to stop. It feels right... ***Do that only which is right.***

As I finish the job, all falls silent and the only thing I can do is smile smugly to myself. I did it. Despite all my doubts and worries, I did it. I am brave. I am strong. I feel accomplished.

I look at what I achieved. It's covered in blood and still bleeding. I no longer recognize it... It doesn't look anything like it used to. The world around me slowly fades until all my attention is on it... Nothing fills my mind asides from memories...

I'm 12 and he's holding me as I cry, rocking back forth. He whispers in my ear that everything will be okay. I clutch his shoulders as he runs his fingers through my long hair.

With a flicker of firefly in the night – I'm three. He's with me, laughing as he knocks down my block tower. I yell at him, placing my hands on my hips and stomping my feet. His face becomes sad as he tries to hug me – a six-year-old's attempt at an apology. I push him away.

A crack of thunder and I'm eight – trapped in a bus-stop during a hurricane. My heart is pounding and all I want is to hug my mommy who should have been there on the last bus. Bentley appears, smiling before me and offers his rain-jacket. I take it and smile as he sits next to me, placing his arm around me as his mother kindly explains that my mother's bus was canceled and I'll be staying with them for the night.

A crow squawks – and I'm fourteen in Bentley's car on Halloween. *You Belong With Me* by Taylor Swift flashes on the radio and Bentley looks at me with his intense eyes, telling me that I'm beautiful in his own way. He leans toward me and I can't breathe. I know what's coming. His lips touch mine, but before I can enjoy our first kiss, I am brought back to reality.

His mutilated body lies in front of me. Realization washes over me as my heart tells me I have known him my entire life. I think about what I did to him just a few minutes ago, and I don't know how to feel.

A slow clap interrupts my train of thought. I turn my head

to see Elijah sauntering towards me, wearing a proud smile upon his narrow face. Star strides beside him, loyal... as if she's his dog and not mine.

"I didn't think you had it in you," he admits as he stops in front of me. Star wags her tail approvingly as she sniffs the dead body.

"I'm impressed, but not really surprised. After all, we have a connection. I knew you'd come through one way or another."

I don't know what to say. I can hardly believe what I've done, and I certainly don't know what I should do next.

As if he can read my thoughts, Elijah asks, "Are you okay?" He peers into my eyes, resting a hand on my shoulder.

"I feel like I shouldn't be... like I should feel regret or remorse. But, I don't. It's rejuvenating in a way," I say in a small, uncertain voice.

"That's the adrenaline," Elijah says smoothly, offering out his hand. I take it and he helps me to my feet.

"You need rest. Go home and I'll take care of this," he promises, kissing my forehead. I nod absentmindedly and start to walk away, happy that I know the way home by heart – I don't think I can concentrate on anything right now.

"Go with Mel," I hear Elijah command Star. "She's earned you," he adds. The jingle of Star's collar follows along behind me as she follows me home. The moon lights my path and offers some comfort in the dark night.

Soon, I reach my window and crawl through it. I can't think. I can't feel. My whole heart is numb and all I want is to be in my warm bed, wrapped up in the protective shield of blankets. I never want the sun to come up. I can't handle the thought of facing the day.

A man lurks in the darkest shadows of my room. I catch a glimpse of him through the corner of my eye.

"Elijah?" I ask, feeling around for the light switch.

The man steps into the moonlight and I freeze. My lungs stop working and my heart goes into overdrive. He's not Elijah at all. He's old and weak. His white hair is nearly all gone from his head. His breathing is heavy and his skin is bruised and blotchy, thinly stretched across his bones. His eyes are deep in their sockets, nearly drained of all life.

"Don't trust him, Mel. There are things you don't yet know," he says through strained breath. I can't take my eyes off of him. I feel my blood rush away from my head and my skin turn cold. I try to scream, but nothing comes out.

Chapter Nine
Do that only which is right

"Granddad?" I manage to breathe out – but by then, he's already gone. I feel as though I've seen a ghost, and I wonder if indeed I have. Maybe it was just my imagination... After all, if it was my Granddad, why didn't he stay? Why didn't he explain more? And why wouldn't he have come to be before now?

I climb into my bed, Star's already resting at the foot. I allow myself to drift into a deep, dark, vast world of nothingness.

I fight against the morning sun rays that pull at my eyelids to open. More than anything I want to stay in bed for the rest of my life... not one part of me wants to face the day... face my mother... hear the news of what happened to Bentley. I just want to stay tucked away in my safe haven of blankets wrapped tightly around me in a cocoon.

I close my eyes, but my mind starts to race. I can feel his presence in my room. In the still of the stale air, in the heat of the silence, I can hear him breathing. I open my eyes, but it makes no difference. When I shut my eyes again, I feel him hovering over me. I pretend I'm still asleep, and try to tell my brain to shut off – I don't want to remember what I did last night. I don't want to picture the looks on Bentley's parents' faces. I don't want to think what tragic campfire stories I have created for this town. I don't want to think period. I don't want to think ever again.

Regret plagues my emotions as my pillow absorbs the tiny teardrops that seep from my soul. What have I done? More importantly; why did I do it? The terrible thing is, I can't even remember. All I know is that I had a reason before and during.

"Girl, why are you crying?"

"Shut the fuck up!" I screamed, leaping from my bed, waving my finger at Elijah's face. "Just shut up, okay?"

"You know, you should be celebrating. You proved

yourself."

"To who? To you? You think I need to prove myself to you? Why would I eve-"

"Well, you must have thought so because it's exactly why you did what you did," Elijah retorted, again it was as if he could read my mind.

"Shut up!"

"You're scared," he stated slowly, his eyebrows scrunched together in a fit of confusion, "something scared you?"

"Killing my *boyfriend* scared me, you insensitive prick!"

"Mel, you need to calm down. Your mother will hear and that wouldn't be good for either of us."

"I don't care what my mother thinks or hears! She's a liar! You're a liar! Who are you?" I screamed. My head was spinning and I backed against the wall. I couldn't be around people, I was going crazy! There was no way in Hell I would ever survive this. My fingernails clawed into my palm as I balled my fists. I wanted to pull my hair out and scream in agony – I wanted to take it all back.

"I think you need to be alone right now," Elijah stated; and with that, he was gone. He didn't even bother to try this time – he just vanished in thin air. I tried not to let it get to me, taking deep breath after deep breath. After what seemed like an eternity, I finally made my heart beat at a normal pace.

I sat down on my bed. I wanted to cry, but I couldn't. There weren't any more tears to cry.

"Please help me," I whispered out. I wasn't crazy, I didn't expect a response. *Plink* – I jumped. Goes to show how unfocused I am - a tiny little noise and it's a huge distraction. What was it anyways? I looked around my room, but failed to see a difference. *Plink. Plink. Plink...* then I noticed, the brand-new pack of pencils on my desk were falling off. My window was closed, there was no breeze... no reason for them to fall.

I gather myself enough energy to stand up and walk away from my bed. I neared the desk, but the pencils continued to drop. I caught one in midair and the rest froze. A deadly silence filled the air – I couldn't even breathe. My hand stays still, but the pencil rapidly dances across my school composition notebook.

Do that only which is right

All falls still. I get lost in the words – what does that even mean? How am I to know what is right? Everything feels so muddled!

Killing your boyfriend is not right, a voice inside my head softly encourages. It is different than it has been. It doesn't sound like Elijah at all; it is soothing, relaxing, and oddly reminiscent of my past. It is a voice I would know anywhere – the voice of my Granddad.

"Where are you?" I whisper, begging him to show himself. My heart decides to fly and I forget all my instincts, including that to breathe.

"Right here."

I wheel around, longing to be swept up in his warm embrace – only to find myself face to face with the last person I want to see… Elijah. I can't hide the shock and disappointment on my face, though not for lack of trying.

"What's wrong, my love?" he asks, reaching out to touch my cheek. I freeze, unable to think of the right thing to say. Although I am confused, I know it won't be good if Elijah knows I am close to reaching my Granddad.

"What's this?" Elijah bellows, shoving his way past me.

"Oh, um, it's just--" I stutter over my own words.

"Where did you find this?" he demands.

I take a deep breathe to calm my head, and slowly reply, "it's just a quote."

"Where did you find it?" he snaps.

"What does it matter?" I ask, grabbing it and tearing it to pieces, "it's just a stupid quote. Look, it's trash." I sprinkle the pieces across the floor. It kills me to destroy the only physical piece of my Granddad I have. It isn't my handwriting, so I believe it must be his. I know it is for the best; it is what he would have wanted me to do.

"I can't believe you!" Elijah grips my upper arms so tightly that I can feel my own heart beat against his hands.

"Hey! Let go of me!" I pull away, unsuccessfully,

"Elijah!" My voice is abnormally high pitched. My heart, once again, decides to pick up to its own beat. My mind races with all the things that he might do with me. The one thing I don't think of, is the thing he winds up doing; To my shock and awe, he lets go and backs away from me.

"I'm so sorry, Mel," he says slowly, shaking his head back and forth.

I can't process his words; I can hardly process my thoughts, anything beyond that is too much. After all, how should I respond to meeting the man of my dreams, realizing he knows your mother, not know *what* he is, figuring out he is death and brought back my dog from the deep, dark, dead, and then hear he loves me when I don't want to see him again?... not to mention somehow being brainwashed to kill your boyfriend! Is that what happened? Was I brainwashed? No... maybe hypnotized? It isn't like I did it willingly... consciously... I can't even think of the right words. This is too much!

"I can't," I scream and suddenly can't control my breathing.

"You can't what, Mel?" he asks.

"Stop saying my name!" My fingers entangle themselves in my hair. The tension feels good against my head, so I pull harder. I want it out! All of it!

Calm down, sweetheart, the voice in my head urges. My Granddad is with me now... Why the fuck am I hearing voices? No, why the fuck am I hearing voices of dead people?! What is happening to me? Who am I becoming?

"Mel?"

"I told you to stop!" I turn around, facing the wall.

"What's wrong?"

"I can't handle it! Make it stop!" I beg, whirling around only to find Elijah gone and my mother standing by the door.

"Mom!" I exclaim, running toward her. I need one of her put-the-world-on-pause hugs.

"Oh, Mel, I'm so sorry about Bentley," she says,

holding me tighter.

"You know?" I ask.

"Of course, it's all over the news!"

I don't know what to say, so I don't say anything at all.

"When did you get back?" my mom asks. I don't know what she's talking about, and I can't process an answer.

"I've been here a while," I say.

"I can imagine you wanted to come home after finding out. Jessica's mom called me earlier, saying you were on your way. If you'd only called, I would've come and picked you up."

"It's not that far," I say, not sure how to respond. What is happening? Is my mom going crazy? This must be Elijah's handy work. I silently curse him out in my head, gripping my mom tighter.

"How did you find out?"

After a mini-heart attack in trying to decide what to say, I reply, "The same You just don't usually watch the news."

Sobs fill the air.

"I just can't imagine who would do a thing like this! And in our small town too," my mother declares. And with that, a gutball rises from my stomach and rests in my throat. I can't say anything. I can hardly speak. *I* am that person. What will happen to me? I don't want to be around my mom anymore. I don't think I will ever be able to look her in the eyes again. What would she think of me if she knew? Surely she wouldn't love me anymore. She'd think I am a monster. How could I have let her down? No matter how hard I think, I know there is no way to make this right.

"Mel?" she whispers softly in my ear.

"Yes?"

"I need to ask you something very important."

I nod. *Here it comes*, I think. How does she already suspect me? I guess mothers really do know everything.

"Do you know what Bentley was doing out there?"
I take in a breath of relief. She doesn't know!

"No," I reply, "we broke up and haven't talked in days."

My mother purses her lips and solemnly nods.

"I understand. But you need to be prepared; the police have already called and wish to speak to you about this later today."

"Why?" I ask too quickly, my heart jolting sporadically.

"Well, you were his girlfriend for a long time."

I nod. I guess I understand, but what will I say? What will happen if they find out? There are so many unanswered questions – who can I possibly confide in? The answer is no one.

"I think I need to be alone," I say, swallowing hard.

My mom pulls away from me and looks into my eyes. I want to squirm out of my skin.

"Okay," she finally says, "if you need anything at all, I'll be upstairs. I called work and told them I won't be coming in today."

"Thanks," I mutter, looking down at my feet. I listen to my mom's footsteps slowly walk all the way up the stairs. Then, I find myself wondering if I will ever walk up those stairs again after I leave for the police station.

I retreat to the familiar comfort of my bed, wrapping my feather comforter around me, calming myself to the sound of my own breathing. In a few minutes, I feel two arms wrapping around me. I want to scream for him to leave, but I am too exhausted.

"It will be okay, you know," he says, running his hand up and down my leg.

"Oh? I'm being brought in for questioning later."

"So?"

"I'm scared."

"You shouldn't be. I already took care of it," he

promises.

"How the Hell can you take care of this?" although my voice is soft, inside I'm screaming.

"Don't you trust me?"

"No," I say strongly.

"Well, I got rid of all your fingerprints and replaced them with a very bad man's."

"How can you do that?" I ask. I can't even put any emotion behind my words. All I want is to sulk in peace and dwell on how fucked up my life has become.

"A thank you would be nice."

"But how?"

"I wouldn't ask questions if I were you," he replies in a tone that suggests he has all the power in the world.

"Thank you," I sighed. Though it pains me to admit it, on some level I do owe it to him. Then again, if it hadn't been for him, I wouldn't be in this mess.

"Much better," Elijah retorted, smiling smugly. I exaggerate an eye roll. He thinks he is God; it makes me sick to my stomach.

"Also, your friend, Jessica, will remember you spending the night last night. So do both your mom and her parents."

This explains a lot about my confusing conversation with my mom.

"You fucking mind-controlling bastard!" I scream. How dare he mess with my mom's memory.

"Easy now, if you wish I can change it back – although it will put you in danger."

I heave a heavy sigh and reply, "Thank you for your help."

Elijah doesn't say anything, just half-way smiles his cocky smile.

"I want you to know that you can trust me. I will always look after you."

I don't care about appeasing him anymore; I scuffed.

"I'm serious, Mel, I'd never let anything bad happen to

you." A pause. "I love you Mel." A longer pause. "I'll let you be, just know everything is okay because of me," he says, and with that he is gone.

I'm not sure how much time passes; everything is muddled. The line between Hellish nightmare and life is blurred, possibly non-existent by now.

It's always darkest before dawn, my Granddad's voice came again. I wonder why he is here – why now? And what does he know exactly? Can he see me?... Hear me?... Know what I am thinking?... How long has he been a part of my life?... and what exactly did he know about Elijah?

I think about all he has said, and I find myself frustrated with the fact that he only speaks in phrases. Can't he just talk to me like a normal person? The quote he gave me repeats in my head like a broken record. What does it mean? Moreover, what does he mean by it? I know he is trying to help me.

Do that only which is right.

Is he simply trying to tell me I did something wrong?

"Mel," my mother's melodic voice rings from outside my door, "May I come in?"

"Yes," I reply.

She walks towards me and sits on the foot of my bed.

"I need to talk to you," she says after a bout of silence.

"About?" I ask.

"Elijah," is her reply.

"I haven't seen him."

"He is dangerous."

"I know, mom."

"Did he have something to do with Bentley?"

"I don't know, mom," I sigh.

"Okay," she agrees, "well, it's time to go. Why don't you put on something nice?"

"Sure," I reply with a shrug, standing. It's like I can't even comprehend anymore; everything around me is dazed and I forget what I said ten minutes ago. Remembering the past few days is like trying to recall the remnants of a childhood dream.

My mother leaves my room in a slow blur as I trudge to my closet doors.

"Boo," the sarcastic voice of my now ex-boyfriend rings. Though it isn't the "boo" that makes me scream; it's his appearance.

"Look at what you did to me," he says in an alarmingly calm tone.

"I'm so sorry," is what I want to say, but it comes out as a high pitched squeak resembling a noise a small mouse might make.

I advert my eyes. I don't want to think about it. He has jerked me right back to my hellish reality, and I remember why I chose to slip away.

"Just look, Mel," he demands.

Suddenly, having no control, I look up at him. His hair is a matted mess, wet with blood. His face is scarred and one of his eyes are missing. I can see his still heart through a gash in his blue polo. Regaining control, my eyes move to the side. Focusing on the wall, his words echo in my hears. I can hear my heartbeat, feel it, and my head is burning with shame.

"Was it worth it? Did you enjoy your adrenaline rush? Tell me, Mel, if you could do it all again would you maybe…"

"Stop it! Just stop!" I beg.

"Oh, but I've barely started," he says, smiling at me as if I am still his perfect little Angel… as if I haven't done anything wrong.

"Please," I beg. I don't know how much of this I could take.

"I'm just so curious, Mel, a sweet little thing like you would never do anything like this. What provoked you?"

"No," I cry, tears cutting my cheeks.

"Perhaps it was that horrid little dog of yours. You know the one, it came back to life. What did that dog do to you, Mel? It changed you… where is that doggie now? Certainly she's not by your side through all this. I don't suppose she ran away? Or did Elijah take her? That is his name, isn't it? Elijah. It has a nice ring to it… if only he did his job…" Bentley trails off.

What is he talking about? What is Elijah's job? How does Bentley know about Elijah?

"What do you know about Elijah?" I ask.

"So, now you're interested in hearing me talk," he laughs. "Well, I'll tell you this. I know a lot more than you think you know about him. But that's not why I'm here. After all, why would I help you? It seems that your perfect Elijah has all the answers... why else would you parade after him like a lost little puppy, preforming his every command. You know, Mel, perhaps Star isn't the dog after all, maybe it's you! You're his fucking little bitch, Melissa, you know that? You're his puppet." Bentley's harsh words drowns in my ears.

"I can't! I just-" my words escape me. I stumble around in the dark. It isn't like I don't want to explain myself, I don't know how. Bentley is right, and it kills me to hear.

"Please just go!" I beg, closing my eyes. To my surprise, when I open my eyes back up, he is gone. I pull out leggings and a sundress, get dressed, and hurry out the door before I can receive any more visits from unwanted guests.

Chapter Ten
The Forgotten

The meeting with the cops goes smoothly enough. She is nice, sweet, and empathic. I'm not even treated like a criminal as I suspected I'd be, and I'm really sure I am no longer a suspect. Although I don't want to, I have to hand it to Elijah – he did a good job at covering my tracks.

"I'm not hungry," I say as my mom offers me a bowl of soup.

"You should eat dinner, Mel."

"But,"

"No buts, Mel, eat something," she insists, her eyes demanding. I give in and force down a whopping three bites.

I can feel his presence as I walk into my bedroom. Memories of him swarm me like mosquitoes on a hot summer's day.

I look up at him as he slowly rocks me back and forth, forcing my eyes to stay open as the bottle in my moth wavers back and forth. He is the first to hold me. I want to tell him I love him; he's the first one I see when I enter the world; he is the first one I know truly unconditionally loves me. Though the connection has been there for less than a month, it's already undeniable. He coddles me, and always will, though neither of us have the ability to see what hard times the future entails, we both know we will always be in each other's hearts.

The memories I tried so hard to forget after his death rush to the forefronts of my mind. I don't know why or how I've seen him so much in my life. I guess after my mother left she kept in touch with him one way or another – making sure we got to see each other. My poor mom, having to leave everyone she loved. I suppose she just couldn't handle leaving her dad. I wonder if she told him about Elijah and that is how he knows now. I wonder what she told him that she hasn't told me – I wonder what my Granddad would tell me if he were physically here right now.

I remember walking toward him as he holds his hands out for me to grab. Walking is new, difficult, and all I want is to hold his hands, standing on my own two feet. I watch his smile widen with each step I take toward him, waddling like a goddamned penguin. I pause to look around for something to hold on to, a table maybe… but while looking I lose my concentration and fall to my butt. Luckily the diaper cushions my fall, but it doesn't help the surprise. It's like the wind has been knocked out of me, I breathe sporadically and can't seem to catch my breath. I feel my eyes start to water and I try and make noise to help me breath.

"Oh, come here. You're okay," my Granddad scoops me up and bounces me up and down in his arms. I find myself calm while our hearts are so close and I wrap my tiny arms around his neck as I my breathing starts to regulate. It's not easy being a baby.

Years later, we return, I can now talk in short sentences and walk. My mother keeps telling me to not touch things as I try to figure out what everything around this new house is. I dart from room to room, exploring each and every thing that rests atop a table or counter, and of course anything that is left for me on the floor. My mother keeps talking to my Granddad, but eventually everything quiets down as they sit in front of the TV. It's not a cartoon, so I'm not very interested. No one is laughing, just watching intently at this leather ball is tossed back and forth across the field.

My Granddad scoops me up and sets me on the couch beside him. I smile and nuzzle my head into his side as I reach for a bowl of chips on the table. My Granddad babbles on about something called "football" and explains to me how it is played. I smile at him as his hands gesture to help him explain. I just want to hug him. Before I know it, I'm being woken up… looking around I guessed I fell asleep beside him. I don't want to leave. I never want to leave him. As my mother slowly pries me from him, giving her goodbyes, I stretch my arms toward him, reaching for him. **Don't take me!** *I think, shaking my hands back and forth. But she does.*

Finally, the most prized memory of him hits me and hits me hard. I feel ashamed for ever forgetting it. Forgetting memories after the death of a loved one is never worth it. I tell myself I never actually forgot it, I just didn't think of it for a while.

He showed up right before my eighth birthday to surprise my mom. I knew though, he told me that he would over the phone. I loved it when he told me he was going to be visiting. I always kept his secret too, never telling my mom. I loved to see her surprised face – moreover, I loved sharing a secret with my Granddad.

The time I spent with my Granddad that trip is blurred, full of fun and laughter. But the thing I remember most is him leaving... I always hated it when he left. I never wanted him to, but I understood that he had to. With understanding, came a yearning to go with him. Being only barely eight, I just didn't understand why I couldn't go with him. He always had to leave early in the morning to return home on time. I loved this because not only was it a chance for me to get up early and wake him, but I knew that he'd spent the most time with me that he could this trip; placing his own deadlines on the backburner.

My alarm goes off at 3:45 in the morning and I leap out of bed. Slipping on my new fuzzy socks Granddad got me, I slip-slide down the hallway to the guest room. I can hear him snoring from outside the door, and I stifle a giggle as it gets louder when I open the door. I always tell him he snores, but he insists that he doesn't; which only makes me laugh more.

I slowly approach his bed and crawl in with him, cuddling up to him and slowly shaking him awake. I love it when the first thing he does is smile. I help him bring his suitcase out to his car as he brushes his teeth. I come in the bathroom as he begins to shave. He shaves every morning, but I keep telling him he should grow a long, white, Santa Claus beard. He tells me that one day he will.

The shaving cream comes out like whipped cream as he presses the button on the top of the can. I smile as he dabs a little on my nose. I wrinkle it, trying to wiggle it off.

Finally, we slowly make our way out to the car, he starts it, warming the engine. His CD player kicks on, and I recognize the song as it rings through my ears. I've heard it with him before. He swoops me up and starts to dance with me. He's like a professional dancer, twisting this way and that, ballroom dancing along the driveway. The song is "What a Wonderful World" by Louis Armstrong, and not only does it fill the air, but it fills my heart as well.

"Take me with you," I beg, though somewhere in my mind I know he can't... know that it wouldn't work out. I just can't help but to ask. Tears stream down my face as I realize that he'll be leaving in a few. To my surprise, he starts crying too. I'm not scared, I know why he's crying, it's the same reason I am. As he spins me around in the early morning, I never want the moment to end. I want the song to play into the day and the next night, never stopping, and I don't want to stop dancing. It's the song that fills my heart now, and always will. It's on an everlasting loop in my memory... it's the happiest song in the world because of that moment... that magic moment... that unforgettable feeling.

My emotions fill me as I search my room for him. I want to see him. I want to feel him. I want to hug him and tell him I love him. I don't know what I would do without him. Though his help is confusing, I trust he has a plan and it will all make sense with time. He is the only one I can truly trust – I only wish I could speak to him freely and openly. I remember calling him whenever I had a problem, or simply needed to talk, and he would somehow make everything magically okay. I remember after his death, clutching the stuffed bunny he got me one year for my birthday and calling out his name, wishing he was there. He is the only person in the world who can fix anything; and I am comforted by the thought that he is somehow here with me now to fix this Elijah problem. My Granddad will always watch over me, help me, and be here for me in any and every way that he can. The tears held back for years to be strong for my distraught mother now rushed forth in an overflowing stream.

"Please," I beg him, "help me get out of this mess!"

Nothing happens, and my heart collapses falling down, down, down into a spiral of black disappointment. My eye catches the corner of my mirror, eyeliner thinned and smeared down my cheek as I reflect on life, my past, and my present – not daring to look into the future. I wish I had never met Elijah. Rage pulsed through my veins; I hate him for haunting my dreams for years on end. How dare he manipulate me in such a manner! And he expects me to love him? To think that I once did is the most repulsing thing to acknowledge. Was it ever love? Probably not even. It was probably just an enforced and manipulated infatuation. I wonder if he even loves me… if not, what does he want me for? *Great,* I think, *more secrets.*

Before now, I didn't know the meaning of hate, or what it feels like to truly loath someone. It's a feeling I want to protect my children from; a feeling I wouldn't dare wish upon anyone. It is the worst feeling in the world and I fear it will never rest, but instead keep eating away at me, gnawing through my hardening heart. I never want to see him again.

Then cast him away, my Granddad's voice flows through my head. It's calm and steady, helping me to relax.

"I can't," I squeaked, spreading the tears on my cheek.

Yes, you can. Believe in yourself, Mel, he urges. I feel my heart lifting again as the anxiety relieves itself from my chest and shoulders.

"How?" I breathe out, regaining control of my lungs and clearing eyes. All falls so silent that a mere thought would boom louder than a firework.

The light around me dims slowly until nothing but darkness surrounds me. Then, a faint glow emits from in between my walls. As if being hand written in a golden ink in perfectly calligraphy, words start appearing on the walls themselves. The energy is breathtaking and far stronger than any adrenaline rush I have ever experienced. The glowing words light up my face as it starts to form sentences.

That is not dead which an eternal lie; yet with strange

eons even death can die.

The H.P. Lovecraft quote echoes in my head, sung my Angels of Heaven. My mind races with ideas. What does it mean? Why is my Granddad saying this? I need help, but this isn't what I had in mind.

Chapter Eleven
True Colors

"Such a sight for sore eyes," Elijah's voice shatters my concentration. Instantly, the quote vanishes and the light returns to normal.

"Elijah!" I exclaim.

"Well, how did it go?" he asks in his casual tone, resting on the foot of my bed. NO matter how hard I try, my heart is set on pumping the blood through my veins in ultra-hyper speed. Did Elijah see the words? How could he not have noticed the weird luminescent light? Perhaps my Granddad has a way of shielding it from evil eyes.

"Fine," I managed to say.

"Just fine? I believe it went fantastically, thanks to me."

"I've already thank you," I stated as blandly as I could, silently adding *which is already too much.* Why is he here? What does he want? My mind trails back to the quote – what can I do with it? I've always hated riddles.

"Mel?" Elijah's voice calls.

"Hmm?" I reply, turning my attention back to him.

"That is not dead which an eternal lie; yet with strange eons even death can die."

"What?" I nearly scream. Panic fills my lungs and bile rises to my throat from sheer terror. What does he know? More importantly, what does he think I know?

"I said, it's getting late and you should get some rest."

"Oh, yeah, you're right," I say slowly. My ears get hot and my cheeks become red with blush. What is going on with me? Am I crazy?... Hallucinating?... this is getting to be too much.

"I have to change," I say, casting Elijah what I tried to make an intimidating glare.

"But of course! I can imagine it would be rather uncomfortable to sleep in those garments, no matter how flattering to your body they are."

There is something about the way he mentions my body that makes me want to writhe out of my skin. Images of him touching me, breathing heavily in my ear haunts me. I can almost feel his unwanted hands on my body, his unwelcome lips caressing my neck. I shudder, shedding the images from my mind. I continue to glare at him until it's painfully obvious he won't be leaving my room for me to change. I turn to face my dresser, my back to him, taking my time to choose my clothes. His eyes bur into the back of my head. I can feel his eyes, mentally undressing me. The last thing I want to do is get naked in front of him. But, I had no choice. There is nothing I can do.

With my back turned, I start to undress, my stomach squirming, being stirred by his intense eyes. I don't like this… not because I think he will do something to me, but because it shows he has power over me; it proves I'm vulnerable.

That's okay, Mel, my Granddad's voice softly whispers in my head, *you just let him believe that lie.* I smile because I know something will soon happen. Although I'm confused, I can figure it out. My Granddad will help me. I can play Elijah's game.

I finish slipping into my pajamas and crawl into bed. Elijah sits above me, running his fingers through my hair.

"My magnificent, Mel," he breathes I my ear. His breath sends chills down my spine and I close my eyes, begging for the gracious world of sleep to take me. I feel something jump up on the bed, and paw at my foot. Star, I realize, and smile. Her energy is weird; her faith lies with Elijah instead of me, and for that I want to cry. She's no longer my Star, but a figment of Elijah's power, an example of what he can do. She is why he acts like he is holier than thou.

"There's something on your mind," he states in a tone that tells me there's no pretending like I'm asleep for this one.

"No," I deny, but even I know it's not good enough.

"Don't lie to me, Mel, I know there's something bothering you. I'm sure if you just tell me, I'll be able to clear it up," he promises, tracing his fingers along my chin line.

"Well, it's just," I start, and then find myself at a loss for words. What do I say?

"Go on," he urges softly, kissing behind my ear.

"What's your job?" I ask, biting my lip. I hope that he buys this, that he thinks this is really what is bothering me.

"Elaborate," he pleads, his words prying me. I know he suspects me, but if I say the right things I can fool him.

"It's just something Bentley said," I slipped.

"Bentley? You've been seeing ghosts?" he inquires. It doesn't take a genius to figure out he's trying really hard to keep his voice calm.

"Ghosts? No, just Bentley. Ghost. Not plural," I try to save myself. I think it works.

"And what did he say?"

"Well, among other things that you're not doing your job. That he knew more than I thought I knew," I say. I wonder if it's bad to be saying this. Surely it's not as bad as if I tell him about my Granddad.

"My job?"

"Yes," I reply, "your job as Death."

"My job as Death," Elijah slowly breaths out. Though I can't see him, I know he's nodding his head, perhaps stroking his chin as he thinks on how to explain this.

"Well, I kill people. Everything has a timer--"

"Yes, you've explained this already. But what's your job? Why do you do what you do… or rather, what you don't do? What's your role, and what purpose do you serve?"

"Could you be more specific?"

"Umm," I think hard.

"It was sarcasm, Mel. Lighten up," he chuckles with an eye roll. I'm not amused.

"Oh," I say flatly.

"My job is rather complicated and cannot precisely be translated. I suppose if I were to put it in simplest terms, I transport souls from one realm to another: this realm to the heavens. It's my job to guide them in the right direction."

I pause, thinking, trying to understand and take it all in.

"And if you don't do this?"

Elijah let out an audible sigh. His hands trembled, moving down my body. "I was hoping you wouldn't ask that. It's very dark, but I will be honest in saying there have been times when I haven't done my job correctly. It's my biggest regret, and I know it will never happen again."

I try to understand what Elijah means, but Bentley was pretty clear that he currently wasn't doing his job. I wonder how much bullshit Elijah thinks he can feed me. There is something about the tone of his voice that makes me want to believe him; something that comforts me and makes me want to be in his arms. It's as if his breath is poisoned, and his words a tranquil spell. His voice and words twists and turns, as he does his best to manipulate me into trusting him. It won't work – though it's difficult to fight to stay in the light, the consciousness, the reality, I will do it. I will do it for my Granddad, my mother, Bentley, and most importantly, I will do it for me. This is my life and I will not be swept away into the blissful naivety and manipulative world Elijah offers.

"If I don't help them, they get trapped in a Ghost World, stuck between realms, imprisoned forever."

"You mean, until you decide to transport them?"

"No, I mean forever. Once a soul is neglected, they will always be stuck in the ghost world. It's the hardest part of my job," he says, his words slow and seemingly full of regret.

"Is Bentley there?" More than anything I wanted to ask about my Grandfather, is this why I can hear him? I can't stand the thought of him being trapped between worlds!

"Of course not, Mel, I would never leave any of your friends alone in that world. The Ghost world is reserved for those who are guilty – it's one of the Hells. The Ghost World is mainly reserved for murders, rapists, those who take their own lives, and other such unmoral crimes."

"And those innocent who you choose to neglect," I scoff, unable to shade the hatred in my voice.

"Unfortunately, yes. And I regret it to the point I am ashamed I ever did such things. I have repented and earned the forgiveness--"

"The forgiveness of whom? What you did was wrong! *You* should be there!" I exclaim, "You are Death! You think you can just stop doing your job."

"You're clearly upset and not thinking right. Your mind is clouded by naivety, exhaustion, and you're overwhelmed. You need sleep. Please, Mel, just close your eyes and we can talk again in the morning. And just so you don't worry, I forgive you for the things you have said to me. Now, you may rest assured."

I want to scream "fuck you, you fat fucking asshole piece of shit," but instead I softly murmur a "goodnight then," because I know there is no arguing with him and it's best to bite my tongue. I know my Granddad would say the same thing. I close my eyes and try my best to forget that he is next to me. I don't want to sleep around him – I'm most vulnerable when I'm asleep, in the dark, wearing practically nothing. But I know I am safe. I know I am protected by those who love me. After all, only unconditional love is welcome in my room and that automatically shuts out Elijah – therefore, he can do me no harm.

Chapter Twelve
Feathers

The world around me is foggy, filled with a blue mist that creeps around me. I can't tell where it's coming from, and I have no idea why it's here. I feel there is a purpose for everything and all will be revealed soon. Everything has a meaning, life, death, punishment, the afterlife, Elijah as the Grim Reaper, and even I have my own place and meaning here. Speaking of, where is here? My eyes slowly undress my surroundings, but I recognize nothing. There is not one thing about this place this looks, feels, or even smells familiar. Everything is different, and my thoughts echo in my head as if I'm speaking into a cave.

     I've never been here before, and I can't recall how I got here. Who is here with me? I sense someone, so I know I'm not alone. I can't place my finger on who's here – there's too many. There's not even numbers here… nothing to comprehend… the closest description I can think of is that I can feel the energy of billions upon billions, possibly trillions. While there are so many, it's like they make up a whole, just one. There's so much energy, it's overwhelming, and nearly draining to feel it all. It's as if they're trying to suck me in with them. No, not like that – it's as if I'm already a part of them, but my consciousness remains, setting me apart.

     I feel like a baby again; it's a feeling I had forgotten until now. Yet, now feeling it, I wonder how I could have ever forgotten? I can actually feel – it's what us as humans try to accomplish with touch. It's clear to me I am in a whole new realm of existence. Am I dead? Did Elijah kill me in my sleep? I wouldn't put it past him, after all, he is Death. I remember being a baby, lying on the floor of my Grandparent's house. I watched things back then… they were… they are my Angels. I could see my Angels as a baby. Their energy felt like this, only on a much smaller scale. I suppose that is only because there were a few of them.

I remember watching them floating above me, smiling down at me, laughing blissfully as they watched over me, keeping me safe. I remember when I used to go to sleep, before I could dream they would take me with them – we would go on fantastic adventures together. They would take me wherever I wanted and we would play. One time, they took me to their father and I trusted him. It felt right, it felt natural, it was the best feeling in the world. What happened? Why can't I see them now? Why did I stop going on adventures with them? When did I stop? I wonder when the first time I actually dreamt was… then I remember. The first dream I had was with Elijah. He stole me from them; he stole them from me.

Where are they now? I wonder if I can see them in this realm. I hope we are about to be reunited. I suddenly can't imagine being without them. They are my best friends, my guardians. They were supposed to keep me away from Elijah, I remember them telling me about him and to stay away. Then, I remember him slowly and steadily gaining my trust and admiration through dreams I thought were this realm. How could he? How could he play me like that? I feel ashamed for ever trusting him over my Angels.

"Do not feel ashamed," the most mellifluous voice chimes through the fog. It takes me back to my adventures with her, the head angel, and my best friend, Charmeine. I look for her in the fog, and she slowly emerges. Her long white dress flows in the soft breeze, flapping behind her. Her beautiful curls are eloquently placed atop her shoulders in such a perfection that she looks, well, like an angel. Her wings are spread open, a representation of trust in their realm. They're white and feathery, with the most gorgeous golden swirls and emblems, each a badge of a good deed completed by her.

"Charmeine," I whispered in awe. I felt compelled to bow before her, but she stopped me.

"I am not above you, but here to help you. The hierarchy is a foolish concept developed by humans. We are all our own energy that makes up one great energy combined. There is no higher power, just us as a whole. This feeling, this is what we all want. This, is what Elijah is supposed to guide everyone toward.

I can't hold it in any longer, if I do I think I'll burst. I take in a deep breath and blurt out "Is my Granddad here?"

Charmeine smiles graciously and reaches out to touch my shoulder. Her touch is the softest feeling I have ever experienced, it sooths my soul in a way others can only imagine.

"Yes, he is here and at peace. Bentley, however is not--"

"Is that because of Elijah, or did he do something wrong?"

Charmeine lets out a flowing giggle and replies, "Melissa, there is no right and wrong. These souls willing go and are put on Earth to experience life. To do what they please and to have the embodiment of free will. They wish to experience touch in a less powerful way, which is why humans are constantly striving for more, yearning for love, it's an experience and you can't have a 'right' or 'wrong' experience as long as something is learned, which is, indeed, inevitable."

"So, Hell?"

"Is a place, sadly, that Elijah created. You see, Elijah is cursed. He is part human, part angel, with access to all realms. This gives him intense emotions, which aren't necessarily a bad thing. We thought it would be good, so he would care about his job – but it had the opposite effect. He cared so much about the people, he watched them, and when they did something he viewed as bad, he would take them too early, or not guide them in the right direction; thus, creating what you know as The Ghost World. It is not his place to judge these souls; it is no one's place. You may only be judged by yourself and your greater knowledge once you return here in this realm. Then you may choose you next journey in Life or, Earth. Judgment is about the scariest emotion one can obtain when in a situation like Elijah is in."

"That's sad," I say, not sure where to go with this. I'm happy to be learning, the mystery is unfolding, but now I have no idea what to do with this knowledge.

"Indeed it is. The Ghost World is where Bentley is, and that's why you can see him. That's why he appeared. That is how he can haunt you," Charmeine explains.

"But my Granddad--"

"His contact is much more limited as I am sure you've noticed. That is because he has found peace here, and is not trapped in such a horrid cell of a realm."

I breathed out a sigh of relief. While it made contact with him and his clues a little more frustrating, I am overjoyed to hear that he is safe, happy, and peaceful.

"In fact, I believe he has chosen to return to Earth one day as your son."

"He can do that?" I ask, astounded. So many questions are being answered.

"Well, of course, but he won't have any of the memories of being your Grandfather."

I nod, showing I understand.

"Why me?" I ask after a bout of silence. It is bugging the shit of me for not knowing, and I hope she can answer.

"Why you what?" Charmeine inquires.

"Why am I a part of this? Why does Elijah want me? Why did he choose me as a baby? What do I have to do with any of this?"

"I thought you might ask that," Charmeine smiles, turning on heel. It's then I realize she's floating. She glides effortlessly across the misty floor. I'm frozen in place, unable to breath, unable to think, completely in awe. Is this really happening? She pauses and turns her head to look back at me.

"Follow me," she says, her delicate voice barely breaking the peace. I feel foolish and ordinary walking behind such a beauty, her wings gently move in the placid wind. I follow her into a room, full of golden stairways, decorated chalets, plates, jewelry with the most beautiful gems weaved inside. And then, a vase full of long, white feathers. This is what catches my eye, and I move toward as Charmeine rests by the door. I stop in front of the vase and lift up on my tippy-toes to peer inside. Are these what I think they are?

"Go ahead, pick one," Charmeine gently cajoles. I breathe out slowly, wondering if I heard her correctly. She is silent now, and I dare not break that silence. I take my time picking one, gazing at each feather as if it is the most precious thing I will ever encounter. I don't touch, until I've found the on meant for me;

and even then, I am careful and slowly place my thumb and forefinger at the tip of the feather, plucking it from its position in the vase. There's nothing different about this one, well, no difference you can see. The difference is the feeling, and this one is meant for me.

I rest it in my palm, and slowly stroke it up and down, feeling each grain touch the my fingertips and a feeling of knowledge fills me. I am taken into a different world, perhaps a different realm, it feels like a dream inside a dream and there is all to be found. I see myself, and then Charmeine, and Elijah is calling to me. I shake my head back and forth, finding myself slipping out of the dream reality.

"Do you know what that is?" Charmeine asks. I look down and see I am still holding the feather.

"No," I reply.

"This is your prophecy. It is rare, but sometimes when a child is born an angel will see who that child will grow to be. Nothing is set in stone, so it's not your future, but we see the choice you will be faced with; the deciding factor in what role you will play in your life. And this, is yours. When an angel sees a child like that, she loses a feather from her left wing. That feather then goes in this room to be treasured until the child comes for it. Does this make sense?"

"As much as it can," I reply with a slight smile.

"Good," she replies. "You are a very special person, with a very difficult choice ahead of you. Do you know what the Angel said when she saw your future?"

"No," I reply, of course I don't know.

"That is not dead which can eternal lie; yet in strange eons even death can die."

That made sense now. Not the quote, but why my Granddad would give it to me.

"Okay," I breathe.

"You are the one who can bring around the balance that Elijah has tilted. You are the only one with that power. You can see the Ghost World and Earth, you used to be able to see this realm and all of us, but slowly Elijah ensured there wouldn't even be a sliver of memory left for you. He took you over in the dream realm, and because of that it is where he is the weakest."

"But what does all this mean?" I ask, understanding and not at the same time.

"It means, Mel, that you have the power to open the portal between realms, therefore setting Elijah free. He'll be able to be in whatever realm he wishes and no longer be trapped on Earth or his Ghost World. This, Mel, is why Elijah wants you."

My mind races with questions, confusion, and wonder. What will happen if I open the portal?

As if Charmeine can read my mind, she answers "if you open the doors between realms, it won't just be these two. There are many realms out there, many different worlds, with many different people, cultures, creatures, and so much more than is beyond your comprehension. If this happens, Earth as you know it, will crumble. The closest translation would be that it could bring about the apocalypse. Not to mention, it will give Elijah the power to draw from those realms and basically do whatever he wishes."

"Okay, so I won't open the door."

"It's not that easy, Mel, if it was, you wouldn't be a prophet," Charmeine warns.

"You must know, if you kill Elijah you will have to take his place and do his job as it was meant to be done. You must be the Sheppard, leading the human souls to this realm."

"And what will become of Elijah?" I ask.

"That, my dear, is up to you," Charmeine says with a smile. The fog starts grow around us, rising. The blue mist conceals Charmeine.

"Wait, no!" I scream after her, but it's already too late. I'm groggy now, flying out of the Angel Realm and back into my dream realm, where I should be. I don't want to leave, I want to see my Granddad one last time, I want more answers, I need these things! But, there is no going back. I must now go forward and make my choice.

Chapter Thirteen
In Death Do Us Part

"Where did you go, my sweet?" Elijah's voice rings in my ears as the world around me creates itself. We're in a field, a field of flowers. Around us there are woods, deep and dark with rainclouds covering them, but we're safe. The field is our haven with blue skies above and green grass all around. The field is as wide and open as I want it to be. I look around to see where Elijah's voice is coming from. Eventually I see him, casually leaning against a tree. As soon as I spot him, he starts to walk toward me, smiling at me.

"Where am I?" I ask.

"You're safe, with me," Elijah replies, taking the last three steps toward me.

"Am I dreaming?"

"You could call it that. Sure, you're dreaming. But this is my world – I created it for you. I need the woods to live, but you like the sun, the flowers, green grass, so I made it all for you… for us. So we can be together, Mel. My magnificent Mel," he voice sings as he spreads his arms out, gesturing to the world around us. He swings me around and around in our sunny dream, dancing and dancing to the birds, and the frogs, the sweet music of nature. I am happy with him. He is my everything. He is what I have always wanted; what I've always dreamed about. He loves me. Everything is happy here, and everything feels right.

"I love you Mel," he whispers in my ear, his warm breath hitting the nerves in my neck, filling me with the most inspiring feelings. Feelings that say anything can happen, anything is possible. The wind whirls around me, singing with joy as I breathe in to return those three little words. As the birds sing and fly around me, I think: *What a Wonderful World.*

Dancing… love… ultimate trust… a wonderful world… my Granddad.

Remember who you are, Melissa. Remember who he is.

You can do this, sweetheart, believe in yourself, my Granddad's voice jolts me to reality, recalling the memories of my life, the memories of my journey to the Angel Realm.

"Mel?" Elijah's voice calls to me. I freeze, unable to breathe and I have no idea what to say. I know Elijah senses that something changed, that something went wrong in his devious plan.

"I-I," I stutter. I feel like I'm falling down into a Tim Burton rabbit hole, with a black and white spiral behind me.

"Don't leave me, Mel," Elijah urges, "stay here with me, be with me. You know I am who you want. I am the right side."

"NO!" I scream, standing from my spiral, planting my feet strongly on the ground. I am determined. I am my own person. I make my own decisions. And I know what I want and what to do.

"Mel, you have the wrong idea," Elijah says, sounding rather empathic. The way he looks at me makes me feel like he views me as a lost sheep, someone he just needs to enlighten… someone he can manipulate. Well, I'm not. I am strong, and I am not a force to be reckoned with.

"Do I now?" I ask, with an all-knowing smile.

"Mel, I want you to listen very closely," he says slowly, articulating every word.

"Listening," I sing back.

"I need you to gather up your powers, your emotions, and I need you to break the barricades against the worlds. You are the one, Mel, you are a special Goddess, and you are the only one who can do this. You're very special, you know your role, I've helped you discover it. After all, I've been here all your life," Elijah encourages, but it does no good. I know where I stand.

"Mel, you've been swayed by the Angels of Darkness… the ones I saved you from when you were little. They were haunting you, corrupting you. They have souls trapped in a realm and they can't get out unless you break down those doors!"

I pause, thinking – what jurisdiction do I have to trust Charmeine? Granted, I don't have much reason to trust Elijah – but if Elijah can do all the mind trick powers, why couldn't Charmeine.

Believe in yourself, Mel. You must trust yourself, and go

with your gut.

My Granddad is right; I need to stick to my guns. Oh, if only he were here right now.

I am always with you in your heart, mind, and soul. I am here with you right now.

I smile, because I know this is true. I can feel this! I can feel him!

"Your Granddad is trapped in there, Mel," Elijah taunts.

"But earlier you sa--"

"Earlier you needed to be comforted so you would sleep."

"So you *lied* to me?" I snapped, outraged.

"Yes, I did. But now I'm telling the truth. Your Grandfather is trapped, and if you release to seal, you release him. Why do you think you could see Bentley so clearly, but not your Granddad?"

"You knew about that?"

"Of course I did, Mel. I know about everything. I am Death, there are no secrets... not even the ones you take to the grave," he laughs a great booming laugh as if he has just made the greatest joke of all time.

"No, you're lying!"

"But, I'm not. I am the way. I am the light. But, you, Mel, you are *the one. You* are the one I am meant to guide, so follow my light, come to me. I will not lie, I have made mistakes, but I realize them now and I wish to rectify those mistakes. I want to do that only which is right; but in order to do that, I need your help. Once those gates are unlocked, I will be able to gather enough power to set right all things in the world, not just my mistakes. I will be able to return my lost souls to the realm they deserve to be in."

"Who gives you the right and power to decide where they deserve to be? You have no--"

"You're right," Elijah says calmly, raising his hands in a defenseless mannerism, "'deserve' was not the right word to use. I am humble and will never judge ones actions. I shall send them wherever they *desire* to be; whichever realm they most wish to be in. Mel, you must believe me, I am the right one, the light against the dark. Knowing what I know now, with everything that I have learned, I would never use my powers for Evil."

Evil is manipulating someone into killing their boyfriend. Evil is making a mother promise her unborn child to them. Evil is Elijah, my Granddad's voice is more prominent than I've ever heard it. My faith lies with him. I know Elijah is evil. There is no way he is good.

"I must admit, you're making a very compelling argument here," I say in an impressed manner. I spread my arms to my side and near him. "However," I add, "I just can't ignore the fact that it's all bullshit. I must be my own judge, and my own guardian. I must trust my own instincts. There is no definite right or wrong, it is a matter of opinion, a matter of morals, and a matter of one's own heart. I must do that only which is right by my own decisions, and everything that I have learned," I explain.

"But of course," Elijah agrees in an overzealous tone, "I wouldn't ever want you to do something you didn't feel is right by your own heart. I'm not at all telling you to do such things, and I sincerely apologize if I came off in such a horrid manner. All I wish for you to do is search your feelings."

"Oh, but I have. Several times over. And thinking back, you have broken pretty much every moral code and ethic I have. Therefore, you are not on my side. What kind of person manipulates, haunts, and forces someone to kill?"

"Now, Mel, let's not be hasty or vengeful here. You did that on your own free will. Just because you regret it doesn't--"

"Enough!" I roar. I'm tired of his babblings. He can bullshit, sweet talk, silver tongue is way through all he wants – as long as he doesn't try it with me.

"Mel, please, you're power hungry," Elijah begs.

"Hardly," I chuckle, "In fact, I'm quite the opposite. You see, I want to set things right, and take away the power from you… the power that you have abused, and the power that you surely would abuse if you were to ever get your hands on it."

"Well, well, look at you, so strong, so powerful. Tell me, little innocent Mel, how do you plan on defeating me? The one you've longed to be with for years? The one you've always dreamed about? The first one you've ever truly loved?"

"I've never loved you!" I spat, "I don't want to be with

you. I have no desire to see you ever again. I wish you would leave my life and never come back!" I screamed at him.

He backed away slowly, gripping his heart. "Oh, no! Anything but that!" he pleads. "If anything, anything at all, be merciful!" he begs. Then, suddenly he stops. "I'm afraid you're going to have to do a bit better than that. All I have is a bruised ego."

My heart starts to panic, skipping every other beat. I'm not getting enough blood, and I think I'm hyperventilating. I feel as though I could pass out at any given moment. I don't know what to do. I didn't have time to plan... or even think about how I might possibly kill him. Is this even the place? I remember Charmeine saying that he's weakest in the Dream Realm. But how?

Easy, Mel, my Granddad sooths, *this is your dream, not his. You can do this. Remember that trick I taught you when you were little? Just look at your hands... then, you'll be in control. Just put him in a bubble, Mel. You can do this,* he coaches.

I take a deep breath and calm myself. He's right, I can do this. I look at my hands. ***This is my dream. This is my dream, and I am in control. This is my dream, I am in control, and what I want to happen will happen,*** I command.

"Elijah," I taunt, calling out in a sing-song voice. "Oh, Elijah..."

He nears me until we are in an arm's length of each other. I lean in closer and whisper in his ear "of all your diabolical planning, your manipulation, and build up to this moment, you forgot one very important thing... this is **my** dream. All these years you've been showing up in **my** dream, when what you should have done is call me to yours. Oh well, I guess now you know; not that it will do you any good," I finish, pushing him back with my hands and he trips into a bubble. It's a giant bubble with the most beautiful blue/green sheen on it.

I look at my hands once more and focus really hard, and soon enough, a knife appears in my right palm. I grip it tightly, admiring the sharp and jagged blade. I run toward the bubble and pop it with the knife – I keep going and it slices into Elijah. The blood pours out, gushing into a puddle on the grassy ground below us. I jam it further into his heart, as he loses his balance and relies on me for support.

"And now, the curse is yours," he whispers into my ear. There is no response, just a thrust of my arm and he falls silent. I take a deep breath and let him fall to the ground. He collapses in a giant heap, falling all over himself. The blood continues to seep out, the puddle growing wider. I don't like killing him, but it had to be done. I feel the blood on my hands start to become sticky and I fall to my knees.

I feel like crying, but I don't. This is for the best, and I know that. So much is gone, though, so much had built to this moment, and now I can't seem to handle it. I see a bright light at the corner of the woods off in the distance. I watch it as it nears me, slowly. The closer it comes, the more I can make out. It's the embodiment of my Granddad, come to see me at last.

"I'm proud of you, Mel. You did what was right. You were so strong through it all."

I can't find the words to say, so I just give him a hug; it's what I've wanted all along.

"I'm always here for you. I'll always be watching over you and your mother. Don't you worry, sweetheart, you and me, we have a special connect. We have something that can't be explained, and nothing, not even death, is going to change that. I love you, Mel,"

"I love you too," I whisper back, never wanting the hug to end.

I see a shadowy figure standing in between two trees off in the woods. A gutball fills my stomach, and I'm brought back to what I am now... who I am. This is me.

"Now, go," my Granddad says, "You have a job to do. I know you'll do it well."

I nod and tears fill my eyes. I notice something I hadn't before, an ocean off in the horizons, the sun is setting into it. Elijah's world is slowly becoming mine as the woods fade around me and the field turns to sand. I feel the spray of the ocean against my face as I watch my Granddad sail off into the sunset, a green flash occurring the moment he's out of view.

I turn back around to the last bit of woods in my dream

and walk toward the dark figure. It's not a human figure, but more of a black blob… it's the remnants of Elijah – it's the true form of his soul.

"I could leave you here," I state. He can't reply, but I know he understands me. After all, I am now the Sheppard and can speak to souls. "I could leave you here to be imprisoned by the Ghost Realm you created forever and not think twice about it… but, that would make me no better than you."

I close my eyes and create the light – the portal to the Angel Realm, giving him the chance to return to where all souls should return; the chance for him to be judged by none other than himself: the chance for him to meet his fate. It was my job, it was what was right, and what should be.

"Go on, Elijah, may your soul live on to better lives," I wish. The blob starts to shake and move, twisting from one form to another, backing away from the silver light. He slowly fades back into woods. He's made his choice; the portal closes.

My death has brought more power than even I imagined… a different kind of power than I ever knew existed… Elijah's voice booms in my head.

"Only unconditional love is welcome around me," I state to the universe. And all falls silent.

I awake in my warm bed, held by cold arms. I suppress a scream and turn to see Elijah's dead body, stone cold and pasty white lying beside me. Star is limp, decayed, and a near skeleton next to him. Her loyalty was his when he brought her back, and it died with him. I am sad to see her go, but her time was long ago. Blood stains the sheets that I carefully wrap him in. I call my mother into the room, and we deal with the body.

"Not a word," my mother warns when we come back into the house.

"Never," I promise.

There's a scratching at the door, followed by a short yip. I slowly approach it, cracking it open something cold brushes against my leg, darting inside. I let out a short, shrill scream, and hurry into the living room where I see Star, part-way decayed.

Worms crawl in and out through her matted fur. She's covered in dirt and wagging her tail over her doggie bed. I cover my mouth as I gag from her stench, forcing the bile back down my throat. I can almost see a smile on her face when I walk into the room.

So good to see you again, Elijah's voice thunders in my head.

The End

19574663R20071

Made in the USA
Charleston, SC
01 June 2013